'Is Gran all right?' I took a small bite of waxy green skin. 'She was a bit . . . odd today.'

'Ouch!' Mum sucked her finger where she'd caught it on the iron. 'She's fine.'

'Is it Grandad then? Is he ill again? I'm old enough. You can tell me.'

'Why all these questions?' Mum started pressing the creases into Dad's shirt instead of smoothing them out. I thought it might be deliberate so I didn't mention it. She still hadn't looked me in the eye.

'Because of the oven chips.'

Alex Gutteridge

Oven Chips for Tea

Corgi Yearling Books

For Isobel, Clare, Elizabeth and Sofie

OVEN CHIPS FOR TEA
A CORGI YEARLING BOOK 0 440 86558 1

Published in Great Britain by Corgi Yearling Books,
an imprint of Random House Children's Books

This edition published 2004

3 5 7 9 10 8 6 4 2

Set in Palatino 12/15pt
by Falcon Oast Graphic Art Ltd.

Corgi Yearling Books are published by Random House Children's Books,
61-63 Uxbridge Road, London W5 5SA,
a division of The Random House Group Ltd,
in Australia by Random House Australia (Pty) Ltd,
20 Alfred Street, Milsons Point, Sydney, NSW 2061, Australia,
in New Zealand by Random House New Zealand Ltd,
18 Poland Road, Glenfield, Auckland 10, New Zealand,
and in South Africa by Random House (Pty) Ltd,
Endulini, 5A Jubilee Road, Parktown 2193, South Africa

THE RANDOM HOUSE GROUP Limited Reg. No. 954009

A CIP catalogue record for this book is available from the British Library.

Printed and bound in Great Britain by Cox & Wyman Ltd.

You always think you know your family. How they'd react in any situation, what they think about certain things, who you can rely on and who you can't. It's not true. Any of it. Nothing is certain.

CHAPTER 1

I knew something was wrong as soon as I looked at my plate. Oven chips.

We always went to Gran and Grandad's for Saturday tea, just the three of us, Nick, Emma and me. Even when Grandad had his stroke and was in hospital for six weeks, we still went.

'It's the highlight of my week,' Gran said, 'seeing the three of you. Besides, it gives your mum and dad a bit of a break.'

Gives us a break too, I thought. An escape from the arguing and the throwing and the 'atmosphere'.

It's been like that for quite a while now. Mum nags, Dad gets riled, they start shouting and then Mum throws something. Nothing valuable or breakable, she's too controlled for that. She chooses her missile carefully – a cushion, or a magazine, or a piece of toast and marmalade. It was my toast and marmalade actually. I eat more quickly these days, otherwise I risk going to school hungry! Then Dad storms out and Mum cries a bit. This is always followed by the 'long silence'. It's like a game they used to play in the car when Nick and I were small –

who can keep quiet the longest. I always used to win and so does Dad.

Gran and Grandad's house is different – or it used to be. There was never that churned-up feeling in the air. Grandad told his jokes and Gran laughed at them as if it was the first time she'd heard them, although it was probably the millionth. Even after the stroke, when Grandad couldn't always remember the punchline, Gran would gently prompt him and then laugh girlishly as if it was some special arrangement that only they knew about. There was always a cosy, warm feeling as you sat around the table and my mouth watered as I waited to see which type of fish Gran would serve with the chips. I like plaice best, but Gran is always fair so Nick and Emma get their favourites too. Then there are the chips, thick, chunky pieces of potato that Gran crinkles herself with a special knife. They're deep fried until they are the colour of ripe corn, crispy at the edges and soft and fluffy inside. Heaven on a plate.

But today something was seriously wrong. The chips had come out of a packet and they lay pale and limp on my plate like bloodless fingers. I pushed the anaemic pieces of potato around and cast a sly glance at Gran, wondering whether to say anything. She looked sort of strange. She was smart as usual, but Gran would look smart if she was a scarecrow! She'd put on her favourite earrings and her blondish hair was as neat as ever. Her face was carefully made up, but underneath the expensive foundation her skin looked slack; the lines that ran from her nose to the sides of her mouth appeared deeper and her keen grey eyes shrank behind puffy lids. I tried not to stare. The expertly applied make-up couldn't mask the truth. Gran had been crying. I'd never seen her cry, not even when Grandad was really ill. A lump filled my throat. What on earth could have happened to make her so upset? I stabbed at a chip and grimaced before it even reached my mouth.

'These chips are soggy,' Emma said in the tactless way five-year-olds have.

I kicked her under the table.

'Ow! Kat!' she squealed, eyes blazing, legs flailing everywhere.

Gran didn't respond. Her mouth just drew tighter and tighter, apart from when she posted a chip through the red-letterbox-type slit her lips made. Perhaps Grandad was ill again, I thought. A chill crept over my heart and down into the pit of my stomach. When I closed my eyes at night I could still smell the hospital. I seemed to have absorbed it, and when darkness came the stench seeped out of my pores. I hated it. And I hated remembering the huge ward with its institutionally tiled walls and matt silver pipes running along the ceiling. But most of all I couldn't bear to think of the pathetic faces as the beds moved further up the ward, closer to the door. For us, the visitors, the door was a way out into the disinfectant-free fresh air. For the patients in this ward it was the door to another world – to death. The nearer the bed moved towards the door the more likely they were to die. I knew it – even Emma soon realized – and everyone in the ward knew it too. It was like the worst-kept secret in the world.

Grandad was four beds away from the door when he was taken in. I hardly dared look each time we visited in case he'd moved closer. My eyes just went straight to the fourth bed down, and even though he had a tube coming out of his hand and his face was all lopsided like a collapsed blancmange and he couldn't speak, I was happy that he was still in the same place. Then, one day, he wasn't. There was somebody different in Grandad's bed. Panic rushed through my body like a tidal wave. I felt hot and faint and sick. I grabbed at Mum's arm, and through blurred vision scanned the beds nearer the door, digging my newly painted purple nails deep into Mum's skin. Grandad always liked me in purple.

'I thought you said he was getting better,' I shrieked.

'He is,' Mum said, 'but it's slow progress.'

'Well where is he then?' I cried.

'He's there' – Nick pointed calmly – 'further down the ward.'

I loosened my grip, as I saw Grandad lift his good hand to wave, a shudder of exhaustion and relief sweeping through me.

'I thought . . .' I couldn't say it out loud. It was bad enough to even have to think it. To contemplate a life without my grandad. Grandad, the person who had taught me to draw, to plant broad beans, to recognize the different types of birdsong, and the person who had taken me along to the table-tennis club and put a bat in my hand before I was tall enough to reach the table! The person who had coached me, encouraged me, swung me round and round when I got into the team. He was the one who kept me going when I played badly, who told me I had the talent to get right to the top.

'Best forehand drive I've ever seen,' he used to chuckle proudly.

And now I was so nearly there, so close to getting a place in the England under-14 table tennis team. Our dream! I couldn't lose him now.

The fear from the hospital ward festers inside me all the time. I must have swallowed it when I ate all Grandad's grapes. It lurks waiting to erupt as it did now, sitting around the table having Saturday tea.

Grandad got up to clear the plates away. He had hardly spoken through the whole meal, but then he had to concentrate hard on chewing and swallowing these days so that wasn't unusual. It was about a year since the stroke and he'd had to learn to talk and walk again. It must have been like going back to being a baby. He still slurs his words sometimes, as if he's had one too many gin and tonics; his right hand doesn't work as well as it did and he drags his leg a bit when he's tired, but he'd put on the weight he'd lost and his skin had lost that greyish tinge. He didn't look ill to me. But Gran did.

She pretended to take an interest when Nick told her about his latest football match, but she had a far-away look in her eyes and I could tell she was just going through the motions.

'Is anything wrong, Gran?' I asked later when Grandad took Nick and Em upstairs to play with his model train set.

For a moment she looked me straight in the eye, then quickly averted her gaze. 'No, love,' she said, moving some mats on the table and then putting them back in exactly the same place. Then, as if she couldn't help herself, 'Why do you ask?'

'No reason,' I said, 'except for the oven chips.'

Gran braced herself against the back of a chair, her eyes blinking rapidly. 'I'm sorry!'

'It doesn't matter,' I said. There was a horrible sour taste of ingratitude in my mouth.

'Proper chips are a lot of trouble and . . . I'm a bit tired. Perhaps next week.'

Her face crumpled like a used tissue. We both looked away.

Gran wasn't the type for emotional outbursts. She may be slim and delicate looking on the outside, but underneath she seemed solid and reliable. The drama-queen gene had bypassed Gran and gone

6

straight to Mum, so Nick, Emma and I got the benefit of a double dose of maternal melodramatics. I listened to the hum of the model trains as they whipped around the track, and glanced at the kitchen clock that hung above the window. For the first time in my life I wanted to leave Gran and Grandad's early and it was a horrible, horrible feeling. At least at home you knew to expect the unexpected. Abnormal was normal there and I'd got used to coping with that. Gran and Grandad's was meant to be a safe place, but suddenly it didn't feel that way. As I stood there gazing out of the kitchen window into the January bleakness, hoping that Gran couldn't read my thoughts, little did I know that my world was about to be turned upside down for ever.

CHAPTER 2

'What do you think is wrong with Gran?'

Nick didn't look up from his computer game.

'Don't you think she seemed strange?'

'Quiet,' said Nick, 'that's all.'

'Grandad was quiet too.'

'Some people like to be quiet,' he said firmly.

I ignored the pointedness of the comment. 'Gran looked as if she'd been crying.'

'Perhaps they'd had a row,' Nick murmured.

'They don't have rows.' I moved the bean bag in front of the TV screen and flopped onto it. 'They're not like Mum and Dad.'

Nick sighed and put down the controls. He ran his fingers through spiky, gelled brown hair and clasped his hands together behind his head. 'Well, go on then. What's your theory?'

I shrugged my shoulders.

'Come on, Kat,' he said, giving me one of his glances that made me feel as if he was the older one instead of being eighteen months younger. 'Spit it out, then I can get on with my game.'

'Well,' I murmured, chewing a hateful ginger curl

to try and straighten it, 'perhaps they know something we don't.'

'What about?'

'About Mum and Dad. About our future.'

Nick rolled his eyes towards the ceiling and wrinkled up his nose. It was a carbon copy of Mum's nose, neat and gently turned up at the end. Why is fate so cruel? I mused for the zillionth time. Just my luck to get Dad's nose with the bump in the middle and Mum's spot-you-in-a-crowd-from-a-hundred-miles-away-coloured hair. I'd promised Nick my entire fossil collection if he agreed to a nose transplant but he wasn't having it. At least I can dye the hair when I'm older.

'Married people have rows all the time. Some of them actually enjoy it. I'm sure Mum and Dad would tell us if they were splitting up.' Nick pressed the remote control and the sound from the television blasted in my ears.

'But doesn't it worry you?' I shouted. 'Don't you think how awful it would be?'

'No. What's the point? We can't do anything about it. It's their decision. Anyway, it's just a phase. They haven't always been like this. We'll have to hope they grow out of it.' He picked up the game controls. 'Will you move now? I can't see the screen.'

I hauled myself out of the bean bag. 'You're incredible,' I huffed.

'I know,' he grinned, dimples appearing in both cheeks.

'How can you be so . . . so frustratingly reasonable?'

'It just comes naturally.' He pushed me to one side.

'It's parental cruelty, you know,' I hissed in his ear. 'We have a right to know what's going on. I'm at that sensitive age where bad treatment could traumatize me for years. I can't blame you for not having my insight and understanding,' I trilled in as superior voice as I could manage. 'After all, you do have the handicap of being a boy.'

Nick stuck his tongue out at me.

Emma was making a teddy bears' picnic in her bedroom.

'Want to help?' she lisped.

I shook my head. If only she was older we'd be able to have heard-to-hearts about the 'situation', but at five she was a bit too young to be my personal counsellor. I strolled downstairs, unable to let the subject drop. Mum was in the kitchen ironing, a sure sign that she and Dad had had a major barney while we'd been out. Sometimes I don't know which is worse, to hear them shouting when you're there or know they've been rowing when you're not. Mum always attacks the ironing in a frenzy of post-row therapy. The atmosphere in the house might have been cooler than the polar ice caps recently, but at least we hadn't turned up at school in crumpled clothes for weeks! She didn't look up as I picked an apple out of the fruit bowl.

'Is Gran all right?' I took a small bite of waxy green skin. 'She was a bit . . . odd today.'

'Ouch!' Mum sucked her finger where she'd caught it on the iron. 'She's fine.'

'Is it Grandad then? Is he ill again? I'm old enough. You can tell me.'

'Why all these questions?' Mum started pressing creases into Dad's shirt instead of smoothing them out. I thought it might be deliberate so I didn't like to mention it. She still hadn't looked me in the eye.

'Because of the oven chips.'

That stopped her. Even made her smile slightly.

'Gran always makes her own chips. Says nothing is too much trouble for us. But today we had lanky, manky oven chips and I know that sounds ungrateful but . . . I wondered why.'

Steam spurted out of the iron and we both watched it evaporate as Mum seemed to be thinking what to say next.

'Gran's not getting any younger,' she said at long last. 'Things change. People change. They can't do everything they used to; sometimes they just don't want to carry on in the same way, doing the same things. You'll understand when you're older.'

She hung Dad's blue shirt up on a hanger. It had looked better before. I flinched as Mum collapsed the ironing board with a crash. She put it in the cupboard and banged the door shut. Her shoulders were so tense they were somewhere up near her earlobes. She started bustling around the kitchen, pretending to be busy. I could take a hint. She didn't want to talk about it. I also knew there was something she wasn't telling me and I was desperate to find out what it was.

Laura's my best friend. She's the only person I've told about our 'problems at home' and she's sworn to secrecy. She understands because of what she's been through. Everyone else thinks we're the perfect family. Nice house, nice car, nice clothes, nice foreign holidays every summer and a week somewhere at Easter if we're lucky. Nice, nice, nice – that's our life from the outside. Mum and Dad are good at putting on a show in public – well, they work together, so I suppose they've got to be. You can't exactly have a raging 'domestic' in front of important clients, can you? They always attend school events *and* they sit together, even if they've obviously been rowing in the car all the way there.

Laura's parents don't. Her mum usually sits towards the front of the hall and her dad is always right at the back, as if they can't bear to share the same air. He perches right on the edge of one of the grey plastic chairs and looks as if he feels he shouldn't be there. Perhaps it's something to do with him not being her proper dad. He's really her step-dad, but Laura says she never thinks of him like that because he's been around a lot longer than her biological dad ever was and as far as she's concerned he's much better than the real thing. After the concert or play Laura's dad always gives her a big hug, pushes her fringe back with his hand and kisses her forehead. He looks so sad, although I'm sure he tries not to, and Laura ends up assuming the parental role, comforting him. Her mum pretends not to notice all this while she adjusts her perfectly draped scarf or ferrets around in her designer handbag. Pity she doesn't find some common sense in there amongst all the make-up. Then Laura's dad slips away and waits outside in the car park for Daniel to join him. He never stops for the cup of tea and piece of cake that the school sometimes provides. It doesn't seem fair that he should always be the one to go hungry, but Laura says it's best that way. I can tell, gazing at her cloudy-blue eyes, that she longs for it to be different.

Laura lives with her mum in the old family home a couple of miles outside town and Daniel, her step-brother, lives with his dad in a flat near the town centre. So it's not just her parents who had split, it's the whole family. Daniel's fourteen, going on four, and a complete and utter pain. To Laura he's the best brother in the world though, and all the other girls think he's really good looking, with his slightly olive-tinted skin and dark curly hair. Actually it's a bit spooky, because he and Laura look quite alike even though they're not related, except her eyes are blue and his are brown. I must admit Daniel's got quite a nice smile, but he doesn't use it much when I'm around. It's more of a sneer accompanied by some sarcastic comment. I can't think why. I don't remember doing anything to deliberately annoy him, apart from tattooing his Action Man with biro roses and hiding vital bits of Lego down my knickers, but I was only about four at the time. I suppose Laura and I could be a tiny bit irritating when we followed him around or spied on him with his friends, but he used to torture our Barbies by tying pieces of string around their ankles and trailing them along the ground for the cat to chase. Perhaps he's just jealous that I see more of Laura now than he does, but that's not my fault.

Laura only visits her dad and Daniel on Sundays – her mum doesn't like her staying over. Laura says it's really difficult. At first she used to cry a lot when she went there, but now they try and catch up on all their news and just enjoy spending the time together. She says it feels sort of forced and unnatural, and no one can relax because the day goes so quickly and they want to make the most of every second. There are always things hanging in the air that they want to say but daren't because it'll bring all the hurt up like bile in the throat and tears will well up and set everyone off. I think this is how it will be for Nick, Emma and me.

Laura and Daniel haven't actually taken sides in the War of the Parents, although she admits it might look that way to people who don't know better.

They're just trying to make the best of things in their own ways, and that means putting their own feelings on hold so neither parent is more miserable than absolutely necessary.

I sometimes wondered who I would live with if Mum and Dad separated. And what about Nick and Em? Would we even be given the choice? Laura and Daniel weren't. It must be harder to *have* to choose. The feeling of disloyalty to one parent must stick in your throat like a dry piece of toast. I was sure Em would go with Dad, even though she's still little and Mum would definitely want to keep her. Nick, being the middle one, well, he'd be stuck in the middle for ages, but I expect he'd go with Mum in the end. And me, what would I do? I'd have the casting vote – my choice would be the final verdict on who was the better, more popular parent. I always thought I'd go and live with Gran and Grandad so as not to give Mum and Dad any extra ammunition to hurl at each other. But perhaps Gran and Grandad would feel taking on a troublesome teenage was too much for them, or perhaps they wouldn't want to be dragged into the arguments, or perhaps Mum and Dad just wouldn't let me go there. Perhaps we'd have to move away from the area, sell our house, change schools, lose friends. I anticipated every worst scenario.

Then, a couple of nights after the oven chips incident, I heard Mum talking to Gran on the phone.

I was sitting on the bit where the stairs dogleg and Mum didn't know I was there. It's a good place to settle if you're struggling to get to grips with a difficult piece of homework. Sort of neutral territory that clears your brain. My bedroom's really nice, with yellow walls, a big bay window and even its own little shower room. The only problem is that it messes itself up really easily and it can be difficult to find a thinking space in the middle of the clutter. The conversation started with the usual grown-up chit-chat and then Mum suddenly lowered her voice.

'They'll have to be told soon. We can't leave it much longer.' My ears tuned into her whisper. 'Kat's already realized something's wrong.'

There was a pause as Mum listened to Gran's reply and I heard her breath as she sucked it in between her teeth.

'Do you think it would be better if *you* told them?'

Another pause. I was rigid with tension, afraid that the stairs would creak and give me away, afraid of what Mum might say next.

'All right then, if you think that's the best way. They'll be devastated. I'll have to find the right moment – if that's possible.'

She put the phone down soon afterwards, but she sat for a couple of minutes in the hall, not moving. All I could hear was her uneven breathing and a gentle intermittent clink as she twisted her wedding and engagement rings round and round on her finger. As last she got up and went through to the kitchen.

I sat on the stairs until supper time, just hugging myself and pondering over and over how much longer we'd got left as a proper family.

CHAPTER 3

'What's the matter with you?' Laura whispered during maths. 'You've got a face like a wet flannel.'

'Family problems,' I mumbled.

'Oh!' She leaned over and squeezed my hand.

That's what I like about Laura. She doesn't say, 'Don't worry,' when you're obviously going to, or 'It'll sort itself out,' which is stating the obvious. She's just there and she understands. I lifted my hand to my mouth.

'I think it's about to happen,' I whispered through my fingers. 'The big split.'

I glanced towards the front of the class. The Hawk's eyes had honed in on me like cruise missiles.

'Katrina and Laura, is there something you wish to share with us? Some mathematical revelations perhaps?' Mrs Hawk's glasses slid to the end of her beak-like nose.

The rest of the class sniggered. It is well known that I'm probably the most numerically challenged pupil in the whole of Heywood Secondary Modern. Laura, on the other hand, is the best in our class and Mrs Hawk's golden girl – or she would be if she hadn't blotted her copybook by being friends with me. I looked down at my book and shook my head, hoping she'd let it drop. Fat chance. Once the Hawk smelled an opportunity she was in for the kill.

'I'll handle this,' Laura muttered.

I smiled gratefully. Normally I'd be right behind her, backing her up, thinking of some plausible fib, but not today. I didn't feel strong enough.

'Kat's not feeling too good.' Laura's a really good actress and she put on her most sympathetic voice. 'I was just—'

'She looks all right to me,' barked the Hawk, stalking the desks, edging closer all the time.

I shrank in my seat as long damson-coloured nails drummed up and down on my desk like talons.

'However, I wouldn't be surprised if you didn't feel well, Katrina, because today is the day I'm going to give you all your test results.'

I wanted to sink through the floor. The Hawk scanned the class and the shuffling and sniggering subsided immediately.

'Some of you have done quite well but mostly the marks are very disappointing.' She stared at me with those chilly blue eyes before swivelling round and marching to the front of the room.

A dejected silence hung in the air as she dropped the test papers onto everyone's desks. Mostly she was expressionless but occasionally someone was blessed with a small smile – Matt, Jo, Hannah and, of course, Laura. She left me until last. Deliberately.

'Some of you have not been paying proper attention. Some of you don't seem to have been listening at all.'

She perched on the edge of her desk and scanned the room. If we've done badly, I thought, it's your fault, not ours. Her eyes moved backwards and forwards like a hunter choosing its prey. I willed her to hear what I was thinking: *If we don't understand it's because you're a lousy teacher. You don't explain things properly.* I longed to let the words tumble out of my mouth as they sparred with my trembling lips. But I didn't have the guts. The sensible, cautious genes that I've inherited from Dad were fighting with Mum's get-it-off-your-chest, speak-before-you-think ones. Dad's were winning and I hated myself for it.

The Hawk looked in my direction, caught my defiant gaze. I felt my cheeks flare up and my heart start to pound. I looked down at the inevitable flurry of huge red crosses that scarred my work. It wasn't fair. I had tried so hard to keep up in class. When she called me up to the front for individual attention, which is a sure way of making you feel even thicker than you are, I had tried to concentrate. Sometimes I could follow what she was saying, but more often than not I only grasped bits of it. I used to skid back to my desk to try and repeat what she'd taught me as quickly as possible before it all got forgotten. It was hopeless. As soon as my eyes logged onto those hateful numbers my brain cells went into freefall.

It was no good asking at home either. Mathematical ineptitude runs down the female side of the family, so if I ask Mum her face takes on the look of a doomed rabbit. She does try, but it's no use. Dad is a different matter. He's quite good at maths and can't understand how a set of numbers can induce such feelings of panic. I sit down next to him at the kitchen table and he explains again and again and again. He tries not to get cross, but I can sense the irritation simmering. The whole thing usually ends in tears, mine and Mum's. The scenario follows a pattern: Dad's patience starts to run out; I get tense; Mum gets cross with Dad and I get narked with Mum.

'It's not Dad's fault I'm thick at maths, it's yours,' I shout.

'That's right' – she raises her voice – 'blame me. Everything is my fault, as usual.'

'Katy doesn't mean that,' Dad says in a strangulated tone, trying to soothe Mum and me and quell his frustration all at the same time.

I usually end up slinking out of the kitchen while Mum starts banging pots and pans about as if she's rehearsing for a saucepan symphony and Dad stands there taking the flak. When Nick grows up I hope he'll be a great inventor and make saucepans out of something quiet or at least tuneful. It could improve the lives of thousands of children in discordant homes.

Mrs Hawk was droning on about the importance of her precious subject. I blinked, swallowed, held my breath, but the tears tumbled down my cheeks onto my test sheet, smudging the ink, dimpling the paper. She hadn't a clue what was really important. I felt so tired, as if all the energy had been sucked out of me. I didn't want to sit on that hard chair any longer, trying to understand something I was never going to be any good at. The only thing I was really good at was table tennis. Staying focused on my game was important if I was to gain my place in the England team. I didn't need maths for that.

I stood up and pushed my chair back harder than I meant to. It fell over with a resounding crash that Mum would have been proud of. The Hawk looked startled.

'What are you doing, Katrina?'

'Going home. I've had enough.'

'Kat,' Laura hissed, 'don't.'

'Are you sick?' The Hawk blinked quickly; a muscle pulsed in her cheek.

'Yes.' I tottered, weak-legged, between the row of desks. I couldn't believe I was doing this. Me. Little Miss Average. The sort of student teachers apart from Mrs Hawk don't take much notice of because I plod along not doing anything spectacular but not doing anything excessively abysmal either. I tilted my chin up, felt Mum's genes surging through my veins. Katrina Matthews the Rebel paused at the door, all forty-four eyes fixed on her. 'I'm sick of maths,' I said in a slightly wavery voice. I wanted to wait to see the reaction, but my bravery had overstretched itself and I darted out of the room, shaking like a forest full of sapless leaves.

I half expected the Hawk to swoop after me, but the place was deserted as I stumbled down the corridor and out of the double doors into the watery January sunshine. I leaned against the wall and took great gulps of air before running up the drive and out of the gates to freedom.

The journey home was just as nerve-racking as walking out of class. I could sense people's eyes on me, wondering why I was out of school in the middle of the morning. Mum had told me to take my coat and I wished I'd listened to her. The black jacket would at least have covered up part of the school uniform that screamed 'skiver' as surely as if it was pasted in letters across my chest. I was convinced someone was going to tackle me, ask what I was doing, where I was going, why I wasn't at school, but no one did.

By the time I reached home my mouth was as dry as one of Mum's sponge cakes. Muffin the cat was waiting on the doorstep as usual to welcome anyone who looked likely to feed her. I picked her up and buried my face in her stripy brown fur.

'What have I done, Muffin?' I murmured.

She nuzzled my chin. I took her inside, opened a

tin of sardines for her and made myself a cup of tea. My stomach didn't feel ready for food. I felt exhilarated and scared at the same time. I glanced at my watch and wondered how long it would take for the fireworks to begin.

It wasn't long.

The car screeched to a stop underneath my bedroom window. I heard the key jumble in the lock and two sets of feet pounding up the stairs.

'Katy, are you here?' Dad sounded worried.

I didn't answer. Just lay on my bed and gave myself a couple more seconds of peace. They burst into my bedroom.

'What's going on?' Mum shouted above the music. She flicked the OFF switch on my stereo. 'What on earth do you think you're playing at? The school rang to say you'd walked out of a lesson and not come back.'

Dad put a hand on her arm but she shook him away. He moved over to the bed, sat down next to me and stroked my cheek like he used to when I was tiny. Then he took hold of my fingers and lifted them to his lips. 'Are you all right?' he murmured.

I sat up and flung myself against him, clinging, breathing in his spicy aftershave and soaking his turquoise shirt with torrents of tears and saliva. He just held me, rocking backwards and forwards as if I was still a baby. I sobbed until my ribs ached, and my chest tightened. I could hardly breathe. Still the tears streamed out. I had lost so much moisture I was in danger of dehydrating.

'I want to come and live with you,' I blubbed at Dad.

Mum stood in the doorway, watching.

'I'm sorry.' I couldn't bear to look at her while I said it. 'It's not that I don't love you as much, Mum, it's just that . . .' I couldn't explain.

'What are you talking about, love?' Dad held me at arm's length now and looked into my ugly, puffy face. 'What's all this got to do with maths?'

'I thought I might go and live with Gran and Grandad.' The words tumbled out now, like water breaking through a dam. 'But then I thought it might be too much for them or they might not want me, but I've just decided I want to live with you when you and Mum split up.'

They exchanged glances and Mum walked over to the bottom of the bed.

'I don't know where you've got this idea from—' she started.

'I heard you!' I shouted. 'Heard you talking to Gran and Grandad. I'm not stupid. I know what's coming. I've known for ages. You don't have to pretend any more.'

Mum sank down onto the bottom of the bed. She started to cry too. Dad was silent. Why didn't they say something? Anything. Dread clutched at my insides like a searing pain. I'd done it now, brought everything out into the open when it was probably better hidden. Me. All my fault.

'Katy,' Dad said at last, soothingly, 'it's true Mum and I haven't been getting on very well lately. Things have been difficult since Grandad had his stroke and then there are problems at work. It's just a bad patch. Everyone has them.'

I almost smiled. Typical Dad. The master of understatement.

'But we are *not* splitting up,' he carried on. 'Not even thinking of it. You, Nick and Emma would be the first to know, I promise.'

I snatched my hand away from his. 'You're lying!'

Dad recoiled as if I'd slapped him. He shook his head.

Mum leaned across the bed. Mascara ran down her cheeks. 'We wouldn't do that, Katy.' She sighed and touched Dad's arm. 'We'll have to tell her.'

'Tell me what?'

Then she dropped the bombshell. The thing I least expected in the whole world. The thing that seemed more unlikely than a nuclear attack on our small town.

'Katy,' she whispered, 'it's not Dad and I who are splitting up. It's Gran and Grandad.'

CHAPTER 4

If they hadn't both looked so distraught I'd have assumed it was a joke. The custard-yellow walls rippled through my blurred eyesight. Mum's voice echoed down my ear canals: 'It's not Dad and I who are splitting up. It's Gran and Grandad.'

The words ricocheted inside my head. Everything seemed unreal. Grandparents don't separate. They stay together. They have a duty to stick it out. They're not supposed to do anything unpredictable. After all, they're old. What's the point of going your separate ways after forty-odd years? A pinprick of guilt pierced my thoughts. I should have felt relieved. My parents weren't splitting, for now at least. But all I could think about was Gran and Grandad.

'Why?' I gasped.

'Grandad wants to go and live abroad.' Dad replied.

The nightmare was getting worse. 'Where?'

'Spain.'

I had the sudden urge to laugh. 'Spain!' It was unbelievable. 'Grandad doesn't like the heat and he's not a beach person at all and we all know he's not keen on foreign food. You just can't get Melton Mowbray pork pies and decent roast beef and Yorkshire pudding abroad.'

Mum dabbed at her eyes with a soggy tissue and shook her head.

'What about Gran?' I shouted. 'He can't just dump her after all she's been through, nursing him back to health and everything.'

'He's not dumping her,' Dad said. 'Grandad wants her to go with him but she won't. She says she can't leave Great-Grandma when she's so frail, even though she's well looked after in the nursing home.'

'And there's us.' Mum blinked back the tears. 'She doesn't want to be so far away from us and all her friends.'

'And Grandad doesn't mind leaving us, presumably?' I knew it was a stupid thing to say, but I couldn't help myself.

'Of course he does,' Dad sighed. 'This isn't a spur-of-the-moment decision. He's thought about it for quite a long time. Since he had the stroke he's felt depressed, restless. He says he needs to move on.'

Mum buried her head in her hands and tried to stifle a sob.

'How long have you known?'

'Since Christmas,' Dad said, 'but he's been thinking about it for longer. We have tried to change his mind, Katy.'

'*I* haven't tried,' I cried. 'He'll listen to me. I know he will.'

'Oh Katy,' Mum sighed. 'He's changed. Sometimes it happens after a stroke.'

'No!' I shouted. 'He hasn't changed. He's just the same as always when he's with me. Please let me talk to him.'

Mum and Dad looked at me pityingly, as if they thought I didn't understand. I knew those expressions from long ago. They were saved for occasions when I'd broken some special toy and they knew it couldn't be mended but I thought it could. It made me feel about five again and it made me angry.

'What about my table tennis?' I shrieked. 'He wouldn't leave me now, after everything we've worked for.'

'You don't need Grandad for the table tennis any more' – Dad pushed my hair back from my face – 'and he knows that. Besides, he hasn't coached you since the stroke—'

I jerked my head away. 'I *do* need him,' I blazed. 'He's always been there for me. I can't make the jump to the national team without him. It's impossible. He's just not thinking straight. I know I can persuade him to stay.'

Mum and Dad exchanged glances. I could almost see the invisible signals travelling between them. They might not have been hitting it off recently, but they still seemed to have this almost telepathic way of communicating sometimes.

'All right,' Dad agreed. 'I just don't want you to get your hopes up, Katy. His mind really does seem to be made up.'

'Well I'm going to unmake it.' My lips twisted into an unnatural smile. 'Will you take me over there later?'

Dad nodded. I touched Mum's mascara-spotted sleeve and leaned over to kiss her.

'Don't worry, Mum.' I summoned up all the confidence I could manage. 'It'll be OK, you'll see.'

Mum took my hand and pressed it to her clammy cheek. She smiled at me, a soft, loving, thankful smile, but her eyes were blank.

I was determined. Grandad was not going to go away. I would speak to him and make him see how silly he was being.

I would make him stay. End of story.

Laura phoned as soon as she got home. She sounded surprised when I answered. 'You're allowed to talk then? I thought you'd be all buttoned up!'

'Very funny,' I droned. Mum and Dad run a button business and Daniel seems to think it's a funny way to make a living. He's always making stupid comments and passing them on to Laura. 'I expect that's one of Daniel's masterpieces.'

'Seriously, Kat' – I could almost smell her

chewing-gum breath as she fretted down the phone – 'are you OK? You whirled out of class like a tornado. Mrs Hawk didn't know what to do. Did you really feel ill?'

'Like I said, I'm sick of maths.'

There was an awed silence from the telephone.

'Did you really say that? Is that what you muttered when you left the room? We couldn't catch the words.'

I couldn't believe it. My one moment of pathetic rebellion and nobody had heard.

'What happened after I'd left?'

'Well, nothing for a while,' Laura replied. 'The Hawk carried on with the lesson, but she was definitely flustered. We thought you'd gone to the cloakroom and you'd be back. You didn't take your rucksack with you. Then she got paler and paler and her face got more pinched looking and worried. In the end she sent out a search party to look for you. I think she's in trouble with the head for not reporting it straight away.'

'Serves her right,' I laughed.

'Are your parents mad that you just walked out like that?'

'I don't think so.'

'Haven't they grounded you?' Laura sounded a bit put out.

'Actually, I don't know. Mum and Dad haven't said much about it really. We've had other things to discuss . . .' A bubble of breath caught in my throat. I paused, swallowed. 'More important things.'

'What?'

I loosened my grip on the telephone slightly and looked at the little gaping holes in the mouthpiece. Tiny tunnels taking my words to Laura. Suddenly I didn't want to talk any more. I couldn't impart my devastating news to a piece of plastic.

'Kat, are you still there?' Laura's voice interrupted the lull. 'Can I come round later? I've got your school bag and I can give you some help with the maths, if you like. I know I'm not very good at explaining things but—'

'Sorry,' I mumbled. 'Table tennis.'

'Are you still allowed to go?'

'Dunno. I suppose so. There's a big match coming up. I really need the practice.'

'What about after that then?'

'I'm . . . a bit busy later.' I knew I sounded off-hand. An offended silence forced its way down the line.

'See you tomorrow if I haven't been suspended.' I waited to hear Laura's infectious giggles. Nothing. 'Thanks for ringing,' I added.

There was a click as she put the phone down.

'Damn.' I banged my forehead against the wall. You have to be ready to share a secret, even with your best friend, and I wasn't. Not yet. Surely Laura of all people could understand that?

* * *

The table-tennis club is only ten minutes' walk from our house. It's actually an old Victorian church tucked in between a row of red-brick terraced houses. Sometimes I cycle or walk and sometimes Dad runs me round in the car. Tonight nobody had said anything about not going, so I changed into my favourite T-shirt and some navy tracksuit bottoms. I wanted to walk even though it was dark and cold and soft rain put a gloss on every surface outside the lead-paned window. I needed time to myself, time to plan what I was going to say to Grandad later.

'I'll pick you up at half-past seven,' Dad said as I gathered up my bag.

'And take me to see Grandad,' I reminded him.

He nodded and his left eyelid twitched, the way it always does when he's nervous.

The darkness calmed me as soon as I banged the front door shut, and the quiet, cold drizzle on my face cleared my head. I composed my speech, rehearsed it several times to the listening trees as I walked and tried to imagine my facial expression as I spoke. I thought the words were short, practical and irresistibly persuasive, my tone of voice sympathetic and coaxing but with just a touch of Mum's I'm-not-going-to-stand-any-nonsense edge to it. By the time I reached the club I'd got it all sorted out. I was confident that soon everything would be back to normal. Perhaps I needed to do my maths while walking in the rain. Perhaps then I'd be a whizz with numbers and Mrs Hawk's beady eyes would widen with astonishment.

The fluorescent lights inside the hall made me blink as usual. I took off my coat and put it on one of the benches that run across the top of the room. There are four table-tennis tables and three of them were already occupied. I sat down for a moment to take my bat out of its cover. The walls are painted bright orange, which makes the room feel welcoming and warm. On the far wall, opposite the seating, there are several wooden boards listing the names of past captains and presidents of the club. Grandad's name appeared more than anyone else's. Club captain six times. Club president for nearly ten years until he had his stroke. Perhaps one day my name would be up on those boards too for everyone to see.

If it hadn't been for Grandad I probably wouldn't have taken up table tennis at all. He gave me one of his old bats to play with before I could walk. I peeled the rubber backing off it and chewed the edges. Then, when my taste buds became more sophisticated, I stopped eating the bat and started to pat the ping-pong ball around the carpet. Soon I learned to totter around the room with the ball balanced on the bat. Grandad did the same with Nick at the same age, but Nick couldn't be bothered to concentrate. As soon as his ball fell off the upturned bat he started to kick it against the skirting boards. Grandad soon went and bought him a proper leather football instead.

Sometimes he'd take me down to the table-tennis club on a Sunday morning. I used to miss more balls than I hit to start with, but he never got impatient and I was hooked.

For my sixth birthday he bought me a bat in its very own case. That was one of the best presents I've ever had. I remember running my fingers around the smooth rim and inhaling the smell of brand-new rubber. I couldn't wait to try it out. Grandad coached me twice a week after that and by the time I was eight I was in the junior team and he said I'd got the best forehand drive he'd ever seen for someone my age. After coaching we'd have frothy hot chocolates from the machine and bars of chocolate or doughnuts showered with sugar – all the things Mum wouldn't let us have at home because of worries about the state of our teeth and the size of her hips. As I got better our expectations grew and now ... I took a deep breath and let the rhythmic *ping-pong* of the balls hitting the table act as a sort of sedative. I was on the verge of a place in the England squad. A couple more good wins and I could make it. I could do what Grandad hadn't quite managed himself, and I imagined how proud he'd be when I got that phone call. I knew it would make everything extra special.

My fingers curled tightly around my favourite bat and I stepped up to one of the tables to make up a doubles match. I wasn't going to let Grandad down. If it meant practising every spare minute of the day, I would. It would be worth it just to see the look on his face when I got the chance to play for England.

Dad was already waiting in the car when I peered out of the doorway. I slid into the passenger seat.

'How did it go?'

'Fine,' I grinned. 'In fact it was better than fine. It was good.'

We sat in silence as Dad drove the fifteen minutes to Gran and Grandad's. I felt calm but Dad was nervous. He grated the gears twice and when he pulled up outside the house the tyre squealed against the kerb.

'Katy . . .' He didn't turn towards me but stared straight ahead through the windscreen, as if he was still driving on past the house. I suppose he wished he was.

I paused, squeezing the door handle tightly. 'Yes?'

He looked at me in the half light and frowned. 'Good luck.'

I walked slowly up the crazy-paved path, waiting in the porch while Dad locked the car and joined me. He rang the bell and a cheerful chime pealed out behind the oak door. Gran didn't look surprised to see us. I should have known Dad would phone to say we were coming – I'd hoped to catch Grandad off-guard. Gran took my face in both her cold hands and kissed me firmly on the forehead. She looked small and old. Her lipstick was all wobbly around the edges and I glanced in the mirror at the pink splodge she had stamped on my skin.

'He's in there,' she said flatly, as I slipped out of my trainers.

They both watched me as I crossed the Wilton carpet and opened the lounge door. Light from the television darted across the dimly lit room but there was no sound. Grandad sat in his usual chair by the fireplace. The newspaper rested on his knee, although it was far too dark to read. I stood for a moment, knees locked, waiting words firmly tethered to my tongue. At first I thought he was asleep. I had to walk right in front of the chair before he lifted his head, but I'm sure he had known I was there all along.

'Hello, Grandad.' I didn't wrap my arms around his shoulders and kiss the top of his head. Suddenly I didn't feel close enough to him to behave in a normal way. The way I would have acted only yesterday. He raised his eyes to mine and in that second all my carefully rehearsed words were spirited away.

'You can't change my mind, Katy. I've decided and that's that.' The only sign of emotion was a slight slurring as he struggled to manoeuvre his droopy mouth.

I searched my brain for the script. The future of our family depended upon what I said next. It had to be exactly right. I couldn't remember anything I had planned.

'Please, Grandad, don't go. We need you here. I need you—'

He looked back at the television. Deliberately cutting me off. A stranger was suddenly squatting inside Grandad. Manipulating his thoughts. Destroying his old feelings. Tears spilled over as I bent down by the chair.

'Why do you want to leave us?' My nails scraped at the Dralon velvet cover, longing to touch his arm but afraid to.

He turned and looked at me so briefly it was hardly worth the bother. With that glance I felt my heart breaking, cracking, splintering.

'How can you?' I choked.

'Because it's what I want,' he said.

'But what about us?' I whispered. 'What about what we want?'

He didn't answer, just stared back at the screen.

'We want you here with us.' I plucked up the courage to grab his hand and twined my fingers though his weakened ones. I had spent hours massaging those fingers after the stroke. 'Please don't do this.' I ached for him to put his arms around me like he used to, but tonight I knew he wouldn't or couldn't.

'I have to,' he whispered. Still he didn't look at me, his eyes were glistening and although there was no pressure from his fingers against mine, he didn't drag his hand away.

Everyone always said Grandad and I were alike. Sometimes we even used to know what the other was thinking. We could finish each other's sentences. But that night I didn't recognize the person in front of me. He was being pig-headed and selfish and distant. Looking at his stubborn expression, I knew that it was pointless saying any more. Nick looked like that sometimes, blank-faced and closed in on himself. I pulled my hand away, stood up and walked out of the room without another word. I was too shocked to cry, too numbed with pain to tremble. It had never occurred to me he could be like this. Cold and cruel. I felt empty, like one of Emma's dolls with the hollow bodies and vacant expressions on their faces. Dad's voice drifted into the hall from the kitchen and I sank onto the oak settle at the bottom of the stairs, unable to face him, unable to admit I'd failed.

I don't know how long it was before Dad came to find me. He coaxed me into the brightly lit kitchen and settled me on one of Gran's smooth oak chairs. I didn't have to say anything.

'I'm sorry, sweetheart.' Dad cupped my hands in his. 'We did warn you.'

'I'll get you a drink,' Gran said, opening a cupboard. Her hands were shaking. 'You must need one.' She didn't grasp the mug properly. It spun through the air, bounced off the edge of the work surface and smashed on the quarry-tiled floor.

'Oh dear!' Gran bent down to pick up the pieces.

'That's the mug you've used since you were tiny . . .' Her voice wavered.

'It doesn't matter,' I said. 'It was an accident.'

She crouched on the floor like a small child looking at the mess it'd made. She started to rock and then to shake. Great sobs punctured her breathing, but there were no tears. I felt as if one of those pottery pieces had sliced through me. Dad and I bent down to try to comfort her.

'Don't worry, Gran,' I whispered. 'We'll think of something to make him change his mind. Don't give up. *I'll* think of something.'

CHAPTER 5

I finally got the lecture over breakfast the next morning. All I'd done was walk out of school, but in the parental book of crime that rates pretty highly. Dad went on and on about responsibility and maturity and letting myself down and letting them down and worrying everybody. Nick and Emma sank so far down in their seats I thought they might disappear under the table altogether. I slumped forwards over my cereal bowl and excavated several holes amongst the flakes of corn with my spoon.

'I spoke to the headmistress yesterday evening.' Dad paced up and down clutching his mug of coffee. 'When I explained the situation she was very understanding.'

I spooned up some milk and dripped it over the cereal mountains. I wondered exactly which situation he'd explained to her: the fact that he and Mum seemed to be on the verge of splitting up or that Gran and Grandad actually were or that I'd been blessed with the most useless maths teacher in the country.

'Well?' Dad barked suddenly.

I jumped, aware that he'd expected some

comment. You can't win with parents. Sometimes if you say something when they're in full flow you get your head bitten off for interrupting. At other times they expect you to make a contribution and help them along with the tirade.

'She could have been very awkward about you just walking out like that.' Mum's voice was becoming shrill. 'She could have suspended you.'

'Sorry,' I mumbled, hoping a sign of remorse might shorten the ordeal. Actually I couldn't understand what all the fuss was about. All I'd done was leave a lesson and go home without signing out. It was hardly like inciting a mass riot of maths haters or organizing a food fight in the canteen. As educational earthquakes went it barely registered on the Richter scale.

'You must not do that ever again,' Dad continued, 'and you must go and apologize to Mrs Hawk.'

'Oh Dad,' I groaned. 'She'll mince me.'

'You're lucky to have got off so lightly,' Mum scolded. 'All you have to do is say you're sorry and I expect you to do it properly. That's not difficult, is it?'

I shook my head. They didn't know what they were asking. This woman would gloat unbearably. She would expect me to grovel. I felt sick. It was going to be totally humiliating.

Laura was in her usual place for a Wednesday morning, just inside the school gates, deep in conversation with Daniel. They don't get much time to see each other in the week. Laura's mum is always there promptly at the end of the day to whisk her home, and she doesn't drop her off until the last possible moment in the mornings. But Laura tells her mum she has to get in early for library duty on Wednesdays. It's a lie, but Laura says she doesn't feel guilty because it's the only time she and Daniel can chat without his mates butting in.

I hung back, watching them, desperate for their conversation to end. Laura stood with her weight on one leg, her ankles crossed and my scruffy bag to the side of her. She was wearing these really cool shoes that my mum said were far too expensive for school. Her white shirt hung out of the back of her blazer by just the right amount and her tie was the perfect length. I fidgeted with my shirt and ended up pulling it out altogether. Daniel's eyes swivelled in my direction. I quickly stared at the ground. My toes curled up into tight little bundles inside my sensible shoes. It's horrible to think someone hates you, even if you're not too keen on them either. Daniel looked back at Laura and inclined his head in my direction. Then he squeezed her arm and strode off towards his classroom. Laura picked up my bag and waited for me to join her.

'Sorry,' I said ruefully. 'I didn't mean to break anything up.'

'You didn't.' I was a bit taken aback by the slight

frostiness in her voice. 'Daniel had something to do. God, you look terrible.' Her tone thawed and she moved closer.

'Something dreadful has happened.' I swallowed hard, struggling to stay composed.

'Kat, what on earth is it?' She put her arm around me.

So I told her. In one of the most public places possible I confessed everything in the hope that sharing it with someone outside the family would help. I didn't look at her face, just stared down at the cracks in the concrete and listened to the words spilling out of my mouth. When I'd finished she didn't say anything, just patted my shoulder. The bell rang, signalling the start of the first lesson. I could hear the hustle and bustle all around us as kids swarmed towards the main building. A couple of bags swung into my side, people called my name – 'Kat, are you coming?' – but I felt strange, as if I was enclosed in a hermetically sealed package that separated me from the real world.

'I'm sorry,' Laura said at last. 'I like your grandad.'

'I just don't know why he's doing it,' I choked. 'I don't understand *how* he can do it.'

'Try to look on the bright side,' Laura said. 'It could be worse.'

Crack! The packaging was ripped open and the thunderous sounds of traffic and school life reverberated through my brain. *How can it be worse?* I wanted to scream, but I couldn't speak.

'I thought you were going to say your mum and dad were separating.'

It felt as if she'd struck me in the stomach. I ran my tongue around the inside of my mouth to relieve the dryness.

'I mean, it's not as if you live with your gran and grandad, is it?'

I couldn't look at her. She didn't understand at all. She wasn't feeling my pain like a best friend should. She could at least have pretended.

'What about the table tennis?' I mumbled. 'I'll never get into the England team now.'

'Of course you will,' Laura reassured me. 'It won't make any difference if . . .'

This time I did look at her, open-mouthed. She bit her lip.

'Look, Kat, I'm sorry, I didn't mean that the way it sounded . . . what I meant was, you can do that by yourself.'

She still had her arm dragged around my shoulder. I pulled away, snatched my bag from her hand and walked off across the yard. Suddenly there was no one I could trust. No one to rely on. Laura fell into step beside me, close, her arm almost touching mine. To the outside world everything must have looked the same as always, but for me a huge chasm had opened between us. I glanced at her inscrutable expression. Didn't she realize the damage she had done?

Overnight I'd acquired a reputation – and not just amongst the other kids. The teachers were wary. They had obviously been warned that I was like a volcano about to erupt. I could see the tension in their bodies, the way they darted glances in my direction but were afraid to make eye contact. I had gained a sort of power, something a middle-of-the-road pupil like me wasn't used to. I only had to shift in my seat and Mr Robinson, my English teacher, was on red alert. In history I dropped my pencil case and you'd have thought a bomb had gone off! It was almost funny. If I'd been a drama queen like Emma I'd have played it for all it was worth. She'd have had all the teachers chucking valium in their coffee by lunch time, but I didn't have the courage or the energy to exploit the situation.

At first break I had to follow Mum and Dad's instructions and flush out the Hawk. She must have been expecting me, but I suppose she thought it was better sport to make me search. I tried the staff room first: she wasn't there, and if they knew her hiding place no one was telling. Then I tried her classroom. Her black jacket with the big gold buttons was over the back of the chair, but there was no sign of her. I was strolling down the corridor, wondering where else to look, when I spotted her through the window. She was in the staff car park, dragging on a cigarette. I dawdled down the stairs with the taste of cornflakes coming back into my mouth, shoved my way through the double doors and stopped. It was so cold the puddles were turning opaque as they iced over. I smoothed down my skirt, straightened my tie, took a deep breath and turned the corner. She stubbed out her cigarette as soon as she saw me, crushing it ruthlessly under her black patent heel.

'Mrs Hawk?'

'Yes, Katrina?'

'I've come to say sorry.' I thought I'd mumble, fluff it, sound insincere, but the words floated out easily and seemed to hang in front of us for a few seconds amidst the little clouds of my breath. I was surprised how calm I sounded, even though I was expecting her to chew me up and spit me out.

Her hand fluttered to her throat and fingered a silver owl on a chain. She seemed uncomfortable. I watched the heat rise up her neck and flush her face. She's about fifty but her skin is perfect. A light dusting of ivory powder and the compulsory red lipstick always gives her features a mask-like appearance. As I waited for her response, beads of sweat blotted the immaculate make-up around her nose. I couldn't believe she was hot. I had pulled the sleeves of my jumper down over my hands to try and ward off hypothermia while I waited for her answer.

'I shouldn't have just walked out like that,' I said.

The muscles in her jaw tensed. She blinked rapidly and pulled herself up as tall as she would go. This is it, I thought, wincing, hunching my shoulders. She's ready for the attack.

'I want you to come and see me at break time, just once a week. We can spend twenty minutes going through all the things you find difficult – just the two of us.' Her voice cut through the chill like an arrow-tip fresh from the furnace.

I hoped the cold was making me hallucinate.

'Katrina?' she almost snapped. 'What do you think? Would it help?'

What could I say – me, Little Miss Daren't-say-boo-to-a-goose-let-alone-no-to-a-hawk? I was trapped. It was the last thing I wanted, a one-to-one with my worst enemy, but I didn't have any choice.

'If you like,' I agreed rather ungraciously.

Her shoulders dropped and her jaw relaxed slightly. My shoulders were making a good attempt to touch my earlobes and my jaw was locked as securely as Nick's money box.

'Excellent.' She seemed really pleased. 'We'll start tomorrow. We'd better go inside. Break is nearly over.'

Her lips curled into what looked suspiciously like a small smile; she swung her bag over her shoulder and clicked away across the concrete. I stayed where I was, shell-shocked.

'And Katrina . . .' Her voice was scarily soft all of a sudden as she turned briefly to look at me. Her expression was weird, almost sympathetic. I had an awful sense of foreboding. 'About what you said yesterday as you left the classroom. Don't worry about it. Sometimes I get sick of maths too.'

She didn't wait for a reply, didn't seem to expect one, which is a good thing because my vocal cords were in serious need of re-tuning. I don't think I could have uttered the tiniest sound, let alone a whole word. She just carried on walking and I heard the rumble of the doors as they swung closed after her. I felt as if I was in the middle of one of those strange dreams where everyone looks familiar but behaves differently. Nothing was normal any more. I wasn't sure what anyone was going to say or do next. I wasn't even sure of myself.

CHAPTER 6

By the time I got home from school Mum had told Nick and Em about Gran and Grandad. Em didn't really understand properly. She knew she'd still be able to see Gran and Grandad, although not together. It didn't seem to bother her too much. She seemed more excited about the thought of regular visits to Spain and rushed upstairs to root out her swimsuit in readiness. Nick wore the flat expression that makes some people think he doesn't care but really means he's buried his feelings deep inside. I knew it was best to wait until he was ready to talk about it.

'I'll miss the house,' he said later that evening as we played on the PlayStation together.

I zapped an alien with a vicious stab of my thumb on the controls. 'What do you mean? Which house?'

'Gran and Grandad's house, of course. They're going to sell it.' Nick crumbled another couple of aliens on the screen. I dropped my set of controls and let myself die.

It had never crossed my mind that the house might be sold. 'Who told you that?'

'No one. I just sort of overheard it.' Nick shuffled in his chair.

'Well, you must have made a mistake. You're always doing it.'

Nick looked indignant. 'Gran won't want to stay there, will she? The house is far too big for one person and she'd never manage the garden on her own.'

'The house isn't *that* big,' I contradicted, 'and she could get a gardener.'

Nick shrugged his shoulders and hunched himself up so I couldn't see his expression properly. 'Why don't you ask Mum, if you don't believe me?'

I glared at his profile. 'Anyway, is that all you'll miss?' I snapped. 'Just the house? Nothing else?'

'Of course I'll miss Grandad too.' He swallowed hard and his bottom lip quivered slightly as if he was about to cry. Suddenly I felt like a prize cow.

Nick swivelled his head around to face me. 'He's not your personal property, you know, even if you are his favourite.' Something flashed in his eyes that I'd never seen before. Jealousy.

'You know that's not true,' I said softly. 'Grandad doesn't have a favourite. He's not the type.'

Nick drew his knees up towards his chin and scrunched himself up into a ball. Guilt washed over me. There *was* a special feeling between Grandad and me, everybody knew that. I'd never thought that Nick might feel left out sometimes. I didn't know what to say to make him feel better so I just left him staring at the TV screen and went to find Mum.

Dad was struggling to extract a stubborn cork from a wine bottle while Mum fiddled about with something in the oven.

'Is it true Gran and Grandad are going to sell the house?'

Neither of them spoke for a moment. The silence crushed me.

'Yes,' Dad sighed at last. 'It's true.'

'Why didn't you tell me? You're always keeping things from me.'

'We're only trying to protect you, Katy.' Dad gave up with the wine bottle and put it down. 'We're just trying to do what's best.'

'Well, it isn't best to be kept in the dark all the time, to think that people have got important things they're not telling you.'

Mum straightened up in front of the oven and pushed her hair behind her ears. 'Sit down, Katy,' she said, pulling one of the pine chairs back from the table. She sat next to me and took my hands between her oven gloves. 'Grandad needs the money from his half share in the house to buy somewhere abroad,' she explained.

'But that's not fair,' I shouted. 'Gran and Grandad have lived there for years and years. You were born in that house. Gran won't want to leave.'

'It's not fair, you're right,' Mum said, 'but there isn't any alternative.'

Dad perched on the edge of the table. 'Gran wanted to sell the house, buy somewhere smaller here and a flat in Spain. She thought that would be a good compromise. They would still have a home here but could spend lots of time abroad too.'

'But . . . ?' I prompted.

'Grandad is determined to make a clean break.' Mum rubbed the bridge of her nose and left a smudge from the oven glove. 'He's just being totally unreasonable.'

'I think he feels trapped,' Dad said. 'There are lots of things he can't do as well since he had the stroke. He has to rely on other people a lot more.'

'But we don't mind that,' I protested. 'Nobody minds that he's a bit slower or had to use a stick sometimes or forgets what he was going to say.'

'But *he* minds, Katy,' Dad said, 'and I think he wants to go somewhere where nobody knew him before the stroke.'

'That's stupid.' I stared at Mum.

'I know.' She nodded.

'So he's turning Gran out of her own home?' I cried.

'She can't afford to buy your grandad out,' Mum said. 'She's got to sell and get somewhere smaller. She hasn't any choice.'

'I hate him,' I sobbed.

'Oh, Katy,' Mum whispered. 'Don't . . .'

She wrapped her arms around me, and as I fought back my tears I felt Dad envelop us both in a big bear hug. For once Mum didn't push him away. We were united. In the midst of my unhappiness I felt a twinge of comfort.

Next morning I overslept. Mum called me three times – I heard her voice through a heavy fog, but I couldn't wake up. My body felt as if Nick and Em had used it as a trampoline during the night.

Eventually Mum had to shake me awake. 'You're going to be late for school,' she scolded, 'and then you'll be in even more trouble.'

I groaned and rolled my legs over the edge of the bed. My foot grazed against the open metal ring inside my French file. 'Ouch!' I shrieked, bending down to rub the red line along the side of my heel.

I pulled on some clothes and searched for the books I needed. Usually I think it's cool that Mum doesn't care how messy my bedroom is, but I do wish she'd make me tidy it the night before I'm going to oversleep. I didn't have time to fill my rucksack neatly so I just shoved everything in, not caring that I couldn't get the zip done up. I walked fast along the frost-patterned pavement, trying to force my hair into a scrunchie and eat a banana at the same time. The rucksack banged against my shoulder blades. The cold air prickled the back of my throat.

'Step on a crack and you'll marry a rat,' I muttered to myself as I zigzagged over the slippery slabs, trying to avoid the lines.

Then it happened. I felt my feet whisked from the ground as if grabbed by an invisible frosty thread and I thudded onto the pavement. It was all Mum's fault. If she'd woken me up earlier I wouldn't have been rushing. If she'd made me sort my books out the night before, I'd have been able to get my rucksack closed. If she'd bought me the new shoes I wanted for school, the ones like Laura's with the sure-grip soles and breath-taking price tag, I wouldn't have slipped. Landing on my bum wasn't the worst thing, although it hurt like hell and my palms were all grazed where I'd slammed them down on the concrete. The fact that my school books were leaning against lampposts, crawling off the kerb and defacing someone's front garden didn't bother me particularly. The worst thing was that when I looked up, Daniel was strolling in my direction.

Please don't let him notice me, I prayed. I sat very still and hoped I might become invisible. I tried this trick at school sometimes. If I saw him lolloping along the corridor towards me and there was nowhere to escape to, like an empty classroom or convenient stairwell, I'd stop and study the pictures on the wall. I was like one of those living statues. Perhaps there's a job opportunity there when I'm older – after all, I'll have had plenty of experience. The trouble is, I'm not very good at it because Daniel always seems to realize I'm there. Once I found myself staring at the fire alarm precautions.

'What's that?' He leaned over my shoulder, minty breath singeing the side of my neck. 'Katrina's got some hot news,' he chuckled to his friends.

They laughed as if it was the funniest thing they'd heard all week. I blushed so hard my face and hair must have clashed horrendously.

Recently, though, we seemed to have reached a sort of unspoken truce. If we bumped into each other when we were on our own he sort of grunted and I sort of nodded in reply and we carried on walking, picking up speed to shorten the moment of contact. Laura was thrilled. 'That's real progress,' she smiled.

'Yeah, right,' I said, raising my eyebrows in amazement. I still didn't trust him. It might have been a little while since he'd picked on me, but I knew he was probably just waiting for the right opportunity and this was bound to be it.

I buried my chin in the folds of my purple scarf, eyes fixed downwards. His footsteps got nearer. I closed my eyes, willed him to walk straight past. He didn't slow down. I thought he was going to ignore me, then suddenly he stopped.

'Katrina? Is that you? Are you all right?'

'Fine,' I muttered into soft purple wool.

'I saw you fall . . .'

I cringed and dug my nails into my black tights. 'I bet that gave you a good laugh,' I snarled.

I heard his sharp intake of breath as he crouched down in front of me. 'You could have really hurt yourself.'

'Not with a bum like this to act as an airbag.' I thought I'd say it before he did.

'Let me help you up.'

'No.' As I scrambled to my feet he jumped backwards. 'I can manage.' I brushed myself down, straightened my skirt and started to march in the direction of school.

'Katrina! Wait!'

My legs wobbled and my stomach felt as if it had been whizzed up in the blender. I thought I'd shaken him off, but no such luck. He caught up with me at the traffic lights.

'Katrina!' He was at my side, grabbing hold of my elbow.

'What?'

'Haven't you forgotten something?' He held my abandoned books under one arm. He was smiling and I felt *so* stupid. He always made me feel like a complete idiot. 'Stand still and I'll put them in your rucksack.'

I stared down the road as he carefully arranged the books and closed the zip so they couldn't fall out again. My back was starting to ache and my palms stung as if they'd got hundreds of needles in them.

'Thanks,' I mumbled ungraciously, as soon as he'd finished. 'I'm late. I'd better be going.'

'Katrina . . .' He brushed my sleeve lightly with a gloved hand.

'What now?' I knew it sounded rude.

'I was really sorry to hear about your grandparents.' He shuffled, looked at his feet. A lump filled my throat, tightness lassoed my chest. His voice was soft, caring and unfamiliar. 'I know how close you are to them. It must be hard for you.'

Don't be nice to me, I thought, not you of all people, not now. I didn't look at him to see if he really meant it or if he was just saying something because he thought he ought to. Either way I knew it would make me cry. I focused on the school gates in the distance, broke into an utterly graceless run and prayed I wouldn't slip over in front of him again.

Mum and Dad were impressed by Mrs Hawk's offer of help. I wasn't so sure. I suspected it could be a trap. Perhaps she just wanted another chance to gloat at my ineptitude. Some teachers can be real sadists.

'You poor thing,' said Laura when I told her. 'That's got to be the ultimate punishment, worse than cleaning the boys' toilets!' She sounded even more sympathetic than when I'd told her about Gran and Grandad. I tried to ignore the resentment that niggled at me.

Everyone dashed for the freedom of the playground at first break, except for me. I trudged along to the Hawk's lair and peered round the open door. She was chewing the end of her pen and staring out of the window. I tapped.

'Yes?'

'It's me, Mrs Hawk. Katrina.'

She beckoned me over to a chair right next to her.

My heart dropped into my feet and I felt all my brain cells following fast. It's soul-destroying being really hopeless at something. Even if you're good at other subjects there's this little gremlin at the back of your brain ready to remind you of your inadequacy and cut you down to size. I was convinced the whole session was going to be torture, but Mrs Hawk must have taken a new brand of patience pill. She didn't shout, or tut-tut, and at the end she asked my opinion. I was gob-smacked into saying it was OK.

'I'm sorry to hear you've got family problems.' She scooped her papers together.

'Mm,' I replied, edging towards the door.

'If you need anyone to talk to . . .' Her hands were ultra-busy, clearing the desk, putting things in her handbag. 'I know you've got friends but sometimes it's easier to talk to a stranger.' She looked up and smiled at me – not the half-hearted lurch of the lips that I knew so well but as close to a genuine smile as I expect she could manage. 'You know where to find me.'

In your dreams, I thought, but nodded anyway. If there were two people I didn't want to confide in it was her and Daniel. They were the least likely people in the whole world to be able to help, or so I thought.

CHAPTER 7

Thursday evenings is team practice. I have to rush home, grab a sandwich, do my homework and get to the club for six o'clock. There are ten of us in the squad and although it's hard work, it's good fun too. Before the stroke Grandad always used to come along and watch. When practice had finished we'd have a quick game and he was never kind to me. If I won it was because he played badly or I managed to raise my game. Afterwards he took me home in his car and we'd discuss my form and areas he thought I needed to work on. Sometimes he contradicted what my coach had said, which was a bit confusing, but I didn't make a big thing of it.

Since the stroke he's been to practice less and less. Mum said it's because he gets tired and doesn't like driving in the dark so much these days. He can't move around the table as quickly and he's had to learn to play left handed because the bat kept slipping out of his right one, but when he does come along we still have a game together afterwards. Even with the wrong hand he can still manage a few mean shots. I know he hates to feel that I'm letting him win, so I don't, but I try not to let him lose too badly. I've seen in his eyes that he knows what I'm up to, a sort of grateful sadness which cuts me up, but what else am I meant to do, annihilate him?

That particular Thursday was nerve-racking. Every time the door opened my stomach lurched and I took my eye off the ball, wondering if Grandad was going to appear. I didn't know how we'd be when we came face to face, and I had no idea what to say to him. My coach must have known something was wrong because she didn't bawl me out for my lack of concentration, but her frown lines deepened as the evening progressed and I knew that although the odd bad session was allowed, it mustn't become a regular thing. Once you start to slide down the rankings it can be difficult to pull back. There are always people waiting to step up and take your place. If you want to get to the top you've got to be totally single-minded, even selfish. That was instilled in me by Grandad.

In the end he didn't turn up to watch. I felt disappointed and relieved at the same time. Dad was parked outside, waiting to take me home. Suddenly I felt exhausted and I slid into the front seat, grateful for the lift. Yesterday's fall seemed to have jarred all my bones and the bruising, aching feeling was taking hold.

'How did it go?' Dad asked.

'I was rubbish.' I leaned my head back and closed my eyes. 'Grandad didn't come.'

'Did you want him to?'

I half opened my eyes and watched the streetlights flash past in a psychedelic blur. How can you want something and not want something at the same time? Thoughts were spinning inside my head, like an out-of-control kaleidoscope. My feelings were like that too, as if they had all been chucked in a paint machine and mixed until everything curdled into a horrible indistinguishable mess. I didn't know what I felt, didn't know what I was supposed to feel. I just knew that whatever Grandad did or said, I wasn't going to be happy any more.

'Anyway,' Dad continued as he pulled up in front of our house, 'you'll see him on Saturday, after your match.'

My mouth dropped open and for a moment did a good impression of one of Nick's tropical fish in desperate need of sustenance. 'So everything carries on as normal. We've still got to go on Saturday and play Happy Families around the kitchen table.'

'I think Gran would like you to go,' Dad said softly.

'What *is* a happy family, Dad?'

He leaned over, stretching out his arms to give me a hug. I ducked, flung open the car door, and made a dash for the house. A cuddle may be enough to sort things out when you're Emma's age, but I'd gone past that.

I glanced into the kitchen before running upstairs. It was the most awful mess. Mum was obviously cooking something special for supper. Whenever she felt life was spiralling out of control Mum tried cookery therapy. I sensed my digestive system waving little white flags along the length of my intestines as I washed my hands. Mum's culinary efforts wouldn't be too bad if she made sure she had all the right ingredients.

'Improvisation is the sign of a good cook,' she said.

'Absolutely.' We grimaced, struggling through Mum's wacky combinations.

She also had a phobia about food poisoning, so everything was cooked well beyond the endurance point of the most persistent bacteria. We had the benefits of smoky, barbecue-flavoured food year long. At least with all that charcoal in our systems the house was a flatulence-free zone. We begged Mum not to bother, told her that our taste buds could live without the challenge of her culinary experiments, but it wasn't any good. Occasionally she had a craving to give us 'good home-cooked food'. Pie-making in batches was her favourite activity and the pies would loom threateningly in the freezer. The trouble is, Mum doesn't always remember to label them, so we'd sit down to steak and kidney pie with carrots and mashed potato only to find it was apple.

'Gravy, anyone?' Nick would ask. 'Or perhaps we could have some custard with our carrots?' That was a sure way to get Mum upset.

'It's a disaster,' she'd cry.

'It's fine,' Dad would say, pouring gravy all over his apple or rhubarb pie, but we all knew it was bound to end in a row.

That night I sighed as we all took our places at the table. Why did Mum have to invite trouble now? Wasn't there enough stress in our lives without actively concocting more?

'What is it?' I whispered to Nick.

'Pasta bake with ham and broccoli.'

I plunged my fork into something green lurking beneath the cheese sauce. It was a Brussels sprout.

'I'm not eating that,' Emma shrieked. 'It's yucky.'

'They needed using up,' Mum muttered.

'No worries,' Dad said, 'it's delicious.'

'It's fine, Emma,' I said, waiting for the ripples of war to churn up the air. Miraculously they didn't come. In between crunching the slightly hard Brussels sprouts we enjoyed intelligent, non-combative conversation. It was quite an effort because we weren't really used to it and Mum was a bit quiet, but everyone tried really hard not to upset anyone else. Emma even ate half a Brussels sprout without the usual gagging noises. Dad cleared the plates away and Mum presented everyone with a chocolate éclair from the fridge. I couldn't hide my surprise.

'What's this for?'

'It's a comforting cake,' Mum said. 'I thought we could all do with one.'

I bit into the soft choux pastry and cream oozed over my lips. It *was* a real treat but it still didn't fill the void that I felt deep inside.

Friday passed in a worried blur. About table tennis, about Grandad and about Laura, who was still not herself.

'What if I don't win the match tomorrow?' I groaned.

'You know you will,' Laura replied. 'You always do.' She sounded tetchy.

'I don't know what I'm going to say to Grandad either,' I mused. 'I've got to think of another way to change his mind.'

'What's the point? You know what adults are like once they've made a decision and gone public. You might as well accept that it's going to happen or you'll only make it harder for yourself. Believe me, I know what I'm talking about.'

I sucked in the mean winter air and felt my lungs press against my chest. Normally if one of us had a problem we'd work it through together. Sympathize, explore solutions, give undivided attention. Today Laura was as cold as the weather. She barely seemed to be listening to me. I'd spent hours hanging on her every word when her mum and stepdad split up. I'd mopped up the tears and tried to say the right thing, even when I hadn't a clue what that was. Now I had an inkling of what she'd been through and I felt she

owed me. Angry, accusing words sharpened themselves on my tongue. I felt like one of Gran's
home-made bottles of ginger beer with the pressure
building up and up until . . .

Some people say rows clear the air but I *know* that's
not true. Rows are like cuts. They scab over after a
couple of days and you think everything's sorted, but
they crack and open up or get picked at time and
again. Horrid, scabby words repeated after weeks
and months and sometimes years. There's always a
little scar left to remind you of the things you wish
had never happened or been said. Somehow I
pushed all the hurt I felt towards Laura down as deep
as I could. If I said what I really felt then things might
never be the same between us again.

That evening I did some stretching exercises before
bed to try and relax, but I didn't sleep well and woke
up on Saturday morning long before it got light. A
blustering wind squeezed its way through the
draughty leading on my window. I felt stiff and cold
and thankful that my opponent wasn't too much of a
challenge. As I got dressed the table tennis seemed to
be the one thing I didn't have to worry about.

Dad ran me down to the club but he didn't stay.
The opposition were late arriving and when we
finally got started I was a bit on edge. It was a nightmare. I couldn't seem to judge my shots properly, my
movements were stilted and my concentration

seemed to have stayed at home. Normally, if things aren't going well I have a conversation with myself inside my head and calm everything down, take control. But this time it didn't work. I could see my coach, out of the corner of my eye, willing me to get my act together. I should have won easily but I threw it away. The other girl wasn't expecting to take the lead and I saw the surprise on her face as she went ahead. All credit to her that she didn't go to pieces. Instead she came in for the kill and there wasn't anything I could do to defend myself.

'You underestimated her,' my coach said afterwards as I slumped on one of the benches. 'It was a silly mistake. You'll have to do better than that to satisfy the England selectors.'

I bit my lip hard and fought back the tears.

'There's still time.' She patted me on the shoulder.

'Not much,' I sniffed.

'Enough.' She smiled. I didn't respond. 'I know you can do it.'

I thought of Grandad. Could I do that too? Could I change his mind and persuade him that he'd made a silly mistake? I wasn't sure, but I knew I'd never forgive myself if I didn't keep trying.

CHAPTER 8

The first thing I saw when the car turned into Cherry Tree Avenue was the For Sale board outside Gran and Grandad's house. It had a picture of two lions on it, with FOR SALE printed above in large blue and white letters. It made me feel sick to the soles of my feet. I expected Emma to make some soppy comment about the pussy cats, but thankfully she stayed quiet. Nick drummed his fingers repetitively up and down on his leg while Mum and Dad sat stiff-necked and silent, pretending the sign didn't exist. The car pulled up outside the gates to drop us off and I tried to catch Dad's eye as he looked in the rear-view mirror. *Please* don't make us do this, my expression begged. He frowned and looked away.

'Come on, Kat, let's go.' Nick nudged me gently.

Reluctantly I opened the door and took my time getting out. As we walked past the board I wanted to kick it hard, but by then Gran was standing on the doorstep, waiting and watching, looking thin and slightly stooped. She smiled and gave us all a big hug. I squeezed her tight and breathed in her perfume.

'Remember why you're here,' a voice said in my head. 'It's for Gran. You're here to support Gran.'

I summoned a fake cheerful face. It felt so forced I was sure it must look grotesque, but nobody seemed to notice. Grandad was in the kitchen, setting the table, and Emma threw herself at his legs, almost knocking him over. He grabbed the back of the chair, chuckling as he bent to kiss her curls. Nick got some glasses from the cupboard and Grandad patted him on the shoulder. I leaned against the sink and kept my head down, desperately wishing I had the sort of lanky hair that fell across my face.

We sat down in our usual places, with Emma beside Gran and me next to Grandad. I wanted to swap places but knew it would look rude, so I just edged my seat a bit closer towards Emma and hoped she wouldn't concuss me with her elbows. Grandad dropped heavily onto his chair. I felt awkward, embarrassed, and I sensed he did too. It was a relief when Gran put the plates in front of us. The fried plaice fillets nestled up to thick, crispy, home-made chips glistening with oil. I slid my knife through the milky-white fish and lifted a forkful to my mouth.

'Great.' Nick grinned, hitting the bottom of the ketchup bottle too hard. A dollop of tomato sauce splodged onto his plate and dripped over the edge like a clot of blood on the white tablecloth. Emma giggled.

Some of the fish flakes wedged themselves in

between my teeth. It's funny how you can suddenly go off something. One week it's your favourite thing in all the world and the next ... It should have smelled delicious, tasted wonderful, the same as always. But it didn't. At least not to me. As I toyed with the food on my plate I knew that for the rest of my life, every time I smelled fish and chips it would remind me of Gran and Grandad and all the happy times we used to have, and how we could have gone on having them if it hadn't been for the person sitting next to me. I folded the grey fish skin over some of the chips and hoped Gran wouldn't notice. Of course she did. Everyone did, but nobody mentioned it. I felt horrible inside. Mean and weak. I knew I should have made an effort to eat it when Gran had gone to all that trouble, but I couldn't.

Pudding was a trifle stuffed with raspberries from the freezer.

'I thought we'd better start eating them up,' Gran said as she spooned the soft, creamy, pink concoction into glass dishes that looked like daisies.

We all knew the meaning behind the innocuous words. Those raspberries were one of the milestones of our childhood. Every June we all helped Grandad pluck them from the prickly canes. He showed us how to apply just the right amount of pressure to ease the fruit from their whitish anchors without squashing them between our fingers. Grandad has big hands with square-shaped fingers, but they were surprisingly deft before the stroke and his bowl always filled up more quickly than ours. It probably helped that he didn't eat as many along the way!

'*One for the bowl and one for the hole,*' Nick used to sing, popping every other raspberry into his gaping mouth.

Emma picked the fruit from the outside canes so she didn't have to lean over and scratch her arms or come into contact with spiders' webs. She was so careful not to squash any fruit that it took her ages. Sometimes we all chatted between ourselves and other times we concentrated on filling the bowls, not wanting to leave one ripe raspberry unpicked. When he thought I wasn't looking Grandad would tip some of the fruit from his bowl into mine.

'My word, you're working fast today,' he'd smile.

Last summer the roles reversed. He was slower, clumsier, bruising the raspberries to a bright blood red, chiding himself as they released their juice over his fingers and under his nails. One day he got impatient with Emma too when she screamed because of a speckled spider, and another time he snapped at Nick for gorging himself instead of putting his pickings in the bowl. After that we didn't talk so much but tried to pick faster and eat less. When Grandad put his bowl down and went to have a brief rest on the bench under the old plum tree we tipped some of the raspberries from our bowls into his.

'See, you're getting quicker every time, Grandad,' we chuckled when he returned.

He'd laughed bravely and his eyes had watered. At the time I assumed they were happy tears, but looking back I think I was probably wrong.

My tears came easily these days too, stinging my eye sockets, souring the back of my throat like the bittersweet raspberry trifle. As the last raspberry slowly melted on my tongue, leaving a gritty residue, I realized we'd probably never go fruit-picking with Grandad again.

Mum and Dad arrived to collect us soon after we'd finished the meal. They stayed for a stilted cup of tea before rounding us up. Grandad and I had hardly spoken. He'd asked me about the table tennis and I'd told him it was a complete disaster. His face was blank. I couldn't tell whether he cared or not. I didn't ask for advice but wondered if he'd offer any. He didn't. When we got up to leave, Grandad stayed sitting in the reclining chair.

'I wish you could stay longer,' Gran said.

'Sorry,' Mum whispered. 'Things to do.' She hadn't looked at Grandad once, hadn't uttered one word in his direction. He had ignored her too. The little lines between her eyebrows looked deeper, as if someone had stuck two staples in her skin. She hadn't bothered to put on any make-up and her face was milky white.

Nick and Em kissed Grandad on the cheek but

Mum walked straight to the door. I followed her, turning just before I left the room.

'Bye then.' I had to say something. 'Are you coming to the practice on Thursday?'

I sensed him struggle in the silence. *Say yes*, I prayed, crossing my fingers. *Go back to how you were before.* Still no answer. I broke into his quietness. 'I've got this big match coming up. Remember? I could do with some of your top tips.'

'You've got a coach for that.' Quick as a forehand volley the words shot back at me. I winced.

'It's not the same.' I heard my voice quaver, sucked in air to steady myself. 'Besides, I need all the help I can get.'

Suddenly he was the sullen child and I was the parent, coaxing, persuading, struggling to stay patient. I knew then how Dad must have felt all those times he tried to persuade us to do things we were unsure about.

'I'll see how I feel,' Grandad muttered.

What about how I feel? I wanted to shout, but I didn't. Gran was already crying softly in the hall, saying her goodbyes to everyone as if she was the one going to Spain. I didn't want to make things worse.

Dad's mouth was set in a grim line as he steered the car round the corner. Mum started to sob and Nick, Emma and I sat in the back like waxwork dummies, listening to them talk. It was as if they'd forgotten we were there.

'I can't believe this is happening,' Mum moaned over and over again. 'How will he manage on his own? He doesn't know anyone over there. What if he's ill again? I just don't know how he can leave the children. I don't know how to cope with it. Any of it.'

Dad passed her a crumpled handkerchief and murmured comforting words when Mum paused for long enough to let him say something.

He stopped the car in front of our black, peeling garage doors, turned off the engine and took Mum's hand. 'We'll just have to hope they sell the house quickly and things don't drag on for too long.'

I couldn't believe what he was saying. I grabbed the back of his seat. How could he betray us like this? I opened my mouth to tell him what I thought, but Nick grasped my arm and pulled me backwards, fixing me with one of his shut-up-or-else stares. For once I didn't fight him.

Mum was crying even more but she didn't disagree with Dad.

'At least now the board's up, they should get some interest.' Dad sighed and ran his free hand through his thinning hair. 'I think they'll find a buyer fairly easily. That really will be the best thing for everyone.'

No! I wanted to shout at them. As soon as the house was sold Grandad would go. How could he think that was for the best? Dad had always been close to Grandad, said he was like the father he'd never known. Now he couldn't wait to get rid of him.

'I can't bear it,' Mum howled. 'I just can't bear it.'

Emma started to snivel and Nick put his arm around her. I knew the house sale had to be stopped or at lest delayed. The more time we had, the more likely Grandad was to change his mind. I was convinced of it. But how on earth could I stop them selling the house?

CHAPTER 9

Emma gave me the idea the following morning. She was playing with her doll's house as I walked past her open bedroom door.

'I need a piece of card,' she said. 'Have you got any?'

'What for?' I asked, crouching down to move a few pieces of tiny furniture around.

'To make a For Sale board,' she said. 'The dollies are moving house and if they haven't got a board outside no one will know it's for sale.'

A fizz of excitement flared up inside me. I gazed into Emma's clear blue eyes as an idea was born. It was something so out of character for someone like me it was exhilarating. If I got rid of the For Sale board outside Gran and Grandad's house it might take them longer to sell it, and that might give me a bit more time to make Grandad see some sense.

'Emma, you are so clever.' I hugged her.

She wriggled away. 'Have you got some card or not? Are you going to help me?'

'There's some in my room.' I jumped up. 'Take as much as you want. I'll play with you later. I've got plans to make.'

While I mooched around trying to work out the best time to commit my act of vandalism, Mum spent the whole day going to pieces. She cried at everything. I offered to hang the washing out. She cried. Nick didn't clear his Lego off the lounge carpet when asked. She cried. Dad said she was to put her feet up and he'd do Sunday lunch. She absolutely sobbed her guts out. It didn't matter if we were helpful or unhelpful, nice or nasty, the result was still the same. My feisty, outspoken, uncrushable mum was like one of Emma's useless rag dolls. The only person who seemed able to do no wrong was the cat.

The worrying thing was that Mum had always seemed to cope in a crisis. When I fell off my bike and broke my collar bone she was calmish. When Nick dropped a whole tin of Airfix paint over his brand-new carpet she was magnificently angry, but she still managed to boil with rage and clear up most of the mess at the same time. Even when the unused chimney in Em's room caught fire she was basically in control. She shrieked at Dad for not having the chimney swept after we moved in and blamed him for the hole in the brickwork that allowed a spark from the lounge fire-place to find its way through. But she organized us all with buckets of water from the bathroom while carrying on her tirade. I never thought I'd say it, but I'd rather have had her shouting at Dad than sitting there sobbing. I think he would have preferred it too.

* * *

It was a relief to get out of the house on Monday. School seemed distinctly appealing and I got up as soon as the alarm went off, grabbed some breakfast and left home as everyone else was just sleepily starting to appear. I'd got plenty of time to spare so I decided to go the long way round and stop at the newsagent's for one of those flapjacks with the thick chocolate topping. As I fumbled in my purse with gloved hands I sensed someone watching me. It was still almost dark but I knew who it was from his shape.

'Katrina!' Daniel leaned across and pushed open the shop door. 'What are you doing here' – he pretended to look at his watch – 'and at the crack of dawn too? Running away from home as well as maths lessons?'

The sarcastic tone made my insides shrink. I decided to sacrifice the flapjack and make a quick getaway. I ducked under his outstretched arm and marched off down the road. He fell into step beside me.

'Sorry,' he said softly after a couple of minutes. 'I suppose you must feel a bit like running away at the moment.'

I bit my lip. 'It's been a bad weekend.'

He didn't say anything trite and I was relieved.

'I lost my table-tennis match and Mum's gone to pieces.' I had no idea why my mouth had overridden my brain and started talking to him. 'She's not in a state about my game; it's because of Gran and Grandad.'

'I see.'

'I don't think you do. I don't think anybody does.' I stopped dead, swivelled round and looked up at him defiantly. He stared over the top of my head and I realized I'd forgotten to brush my hair.

'I *do* understand. I've been through something similar, remember?' His voice was quiet and he stood very still. It was disconcerting.

'Yes . . . that must have been worse than this . . .' I paused. 'At least, that's what Laura says.'

'In some ways it's different, but in another way it's the same.' He looked back at me. 'It's bound to change everything, make people behave strangely for a time. It makes *you* think differently too about people you thought you knew. That's the same whether it's your parents who've split up or your grandparents.'

The sky was turning from pink to mauve behind him. It made his gelled hair gleam at the edges as if it had been henna-rinsed. His eyes were as dark as my favourite chocolate truffles. I sucked in some air with a faint whistling noise and prayed I wouldn't burp. This wasn't the Daniel I knew.

'It's no big deal that you lost the match. It would probably have been more worrying if you'd won.'

I studied his face for signs of gloating but couldn't

see any. He offered me a mint. Suddenly I wanted to hear what he had to say, and to see his expression when he said it. He wasn't talking to me as if I was some silly little girl like he usually did.

'But what about my mum? I mean, she's a parent, she's got responsibilities. She can't just crack up.'

He shrugged his shoulders, looked down and was quiet for so long I didn't think he was going to answer. Then he started walking again and I trotted to keep up with his long strides. Eventually he spoke.

'She may be a parent to you, but she's also someone's child. I suppose it's just as hurtful when your parents split up whether you're fourteen or forty. In a way, perhaps, the older you are, the worse it is. You feel cheated, that all those years they've stayed together have been a sham.'

It seems stupid now but I'd never thought about it like that. Never taken into account that Mum was Gran and Grandad's little girl. I rolled the mint slowly around my mouth. All I'd thought about was myself, with the odd pang of concern for Gran. I felt too foolish and ashamed to say anything. He seemed to pick up on my mood.

'Well, that's only Dr Daniel's diagnosis!' His voice was lighter, jokier. 'I could be totally wrong. It has been known – occasionally.'

I smiled gratefully and suddenly felt tongue-tied. We walked the rest of the way in silence. It felt uncomfortable to have him striding along next to me, his arm occasionally brushing against mine, but he looked quite relaxed. I was sure he'd want to ditch me as soon as we got closer to school, to avoid being seen together, but he didn't make any attempt to shake me off and I didn't know how to extricate myself without looking rude. After all, he had been quite nice, and surprisingly he had made me feel a bit better. He must have thought it was too late to avoid the embarrassment. Several girls had already pranced past us, stifling sniggers and casting envious glances in my direction. I smiled into my scarf as we walked through the gates. This entrance wasn't going to do my street cred any harm at all.

I couldn't wait to tell Laura the plan I'd concocted over the weekend. She was even later than usual so I had to wait until first break. We huddled against the wall out of the wind and nibbled our biscuits.

'I've had a brilliant idea,' I said. She looked keen to hear it. 'It's a plan to stop my gran and grandad selling the house.'

'Oh.' Suddenly she didn't seem so interested.

'If they don't sell the house, Grandad won't go abroad.'

'Are you sure about that?' She sucked at her juice carton so hard the sides caved inwards.

I tried to ignore the seed of irritation that was growing inside me, expanding like some genetically modified monster. 'I'm going to nick the For Sale board. I'm going to take it down and hide it. Then people driving past won't know the house is on the market.'

'You can't be serious.' She shook her head and looked at me as if she thought I was totally stupid. 'The estate agent will give out details and they'll soon put up another board. Are you going to take them all down?'

'No, of course not.' – I tried not to snap – 'but it'll give me a bit more time. I was going to ask you to help. Those boards look heavy.'

She looked startled and I saw it in her face, the backing off, a withdrawal that she'd tried to disguise. I was hurting and it was worse than the bruising from my fall.

'Kat' – she touched my arm – 'you're wasting your time. Just be thankful it's your grandparents and not your parents who are separating. That would be much worse. Believe me, I know.'

'You're right,' I shouted. 'I am wasting my time. You're meant to be my friend and all you do is make me feel like an idiot. Well, don't worry, Laura, I don't want your help any more.' I threw my biscuit straight at her chest and I wished it had been one of Mum's rock cakes. That would have had more impact than a wimpy, wafery biscuit, but she still looked slightly stunned.

We'd attracted an audience so I bulldozed my way through the throng, head down, tears spouting. I stumbled across the tarmac and through the double doors, not looking where I was going. I didn't see Mrs Hawk until it was too late for both of us. As I careered into her, the cup she was carrying lurched towards her chest. Hot coffee drenched the front of her camel-hair suit. I stared at the horrible brown stain and put my head in my hands. Surely things couldn't get any worse?

CHAPTER 10

Mrs Hawk took hold of my elbow, propelled me into an empty office next to reception and sat me down. Then she disappeared for a few minutes. I pressed my cheek against the cool desktop and wondered what my punishment would be. Perhaps I'd have to sign a form promising to endure maths lessons five times a week for the rest of my life, or perhaps I'd be expected to pay for a new suit if the stain didn't come out. I wondered how many times I'd have to empty the dishwasher to earn enough money – it hadn't looked like a cheap and cheerful thirty-quid-off-the-market type of outfit. I groaned and banged my forehead down on the grey metal.

Mrs Hawk returned with a box of tissues and two cups of tea. She'd taken off her jacket and I sat up as she tentatively placed a cup and saucer next to me. Perhaps she thought tea would do less damage than coffee if I somehow managed to shower her in that too.

'I've put one sugar in it,' she said, drawing up another chair. 'Is that all right?'

'I'm sorry about your jacket,' I snivelled. 'I'll pay

for it to be cleaned. Do you think it will be all right?'

She smiled and all her features softened; even her blue eyes lost their coldness. She'd probably been quite pretty when she was young, I thought.

'Don't worry about that old thing,' she replied. 'It's a good excuse to get rid of it and treat myself to something new. Drink your tea. It'll make you feel better.'

I'd always wondered why adults said that. How could a drink make you feel better when the whole world was falling apart? But she was right, it did sort of soothe me. I think it must be the feeling of heat as the tea flows down your throat, behind your breastbone, then between your ribs, before you get this pinprick of warmth in your stomach. It reminds you that you're still alive even if you feel dead inside.

'Do you want to talk about it?' she asked.

I thought for a moment – about how I couldn't tell Gran or Mum or Dad or Nick or Em how I was really feeling because they were all involved. I thought about Laura; about how our friendship was changing, how we'd lost trust in each other. So I talked to Mrs Hawk.

She didn't interrupt once, even when I paused for so long I wondered myself whether there was anything left to say. I told her about Gran and Grandad and how I didn't understand how Grandad could want to go or how Gran could let him. I told her how I thought Grandad couldn't really love me after all, but even if he didn't I still wanted him to stay. I told her about Mum and Dad and the rows and Dad wanting Grandad to go soon and Mum going to pieces and how I felt disappointed because I wanted her to be strong. I told her things that I didn't even know I felt until that moment. How I resented Nick because he accepted the situation and envied Em because she didn't fully understand. How I'd worked so hard at the table tennis all these years and suddenly I wasn't sure whether I'd been doing it for me or for Grandad. How I knew that Laura was right when she said it was worse when your parents split up but hated her for saying it out loud. How I wanted everything to go back to how it was before the stroke, before the rows, before the pain. How I didn't want to grow up if this was what it was like.

I don't know how long we sat there, but I dimly heard the bell go for the end of break and the hustle and bustle back to the classrooms. Eventually I knew that there was not much else left to say. I flopped back in my chair like one of Mum's collapsed Yorkshire puddings and prayed it was all a nightmare. I prayed that I would wake up and find I hadn't confided all my innermost secret thoughts; that all those feelings were still bottled up inside where they couldn't damage anyone except me.

'It's hard being a child.' Mrs Hawk spoke slowly and carefully. 'Sometimes we forget that when we grow up and get all wound up with our own problems.'

I flushed with embarrassment, glanced at my watch and the door, hoping she'd take a hint, that the sermon could be avoided. Fat chance.

'You have to realize, Katrina, it's not easy being an adult either and it's certainly hard to come to terms with getting old or being ill.'

I picked at a loose thread on my jumper. I didn't want to listen. Why do people always feel the need to provide an opinion? Why can't they understand that just getting it off your chest can be enough?

'Sometimes' – she studied her nails – 'sometimes we become trapped by circumstances that we can't do anything about. We're powerless, like children. Your grandad has probably felt powerless since his stroke.'

She hadn't a clue what she was talking about. Grandad was the one with the power. He was the one whose decision would alter our family for ever.

'I'm sure all your family love you, Katrina, and I'm sure everyone is handling it in the best way they can. You've got to be brave. Your grandad is being brave, you know. Going to a foreign country on your own when you're not fully fit is not something many people would risk.'

I should have expected her to take Grandad's side instead of mine. She hadn't listened properly at all. How stupid of me to think that she'd be sympathetic towards me. She prattled on a bit more and I tried to look as if I was paying attention, but really I was wondering where to dump the For Sale board after I'd taken it down.

'Do you feel better?' she asked.

I nodded reluctantly. What's that saying? *A problem shared is a problem halved.* Well, I did feel fractionally better, despite the fact that she'd talked a complete load of rubbish.

'You won't tell anyone, will you?' I stood up, ready to make a getaway.

'Of course not.'

'You won't ring home? I don't want Mum and Dad to have anything else to worry about. They always disagree about how to handle things and then they start arguing.'

She shook her head. 'It's our secret.'

Laura was sheepish for the rest of the day. I avoided sitting next to her at lunch and kept my head down during lessons. I concentrated so hard my brain felt as if it would go into meltdown. When I got home Mum was sitting on the floor in the dining room sifting through old photographs. She obviously hadn't been to the office and barely seemed to register that I was back, let alone have any inkling of my outburst at school. Amazingly, it seemed as if Mrs Hawk had kept her word.

CHAPTER 11

Tuesday was the day I had to take the board down. It would be too difficult to get out during the rest of the week. Laura and I hardly spoke all day, but it didn't matter much. I kept myself to myself and wished the hours away until the evening. By six o'clock the rain was coming down so hard the gutters were overflowing and there was a lake forming on the back lawn. I peered between the wooden slats of the Venetian blinds and cursed.

Dad craned his neck around my bedroom door. 'I'll give you a lift to practice tonight.'

'It's OK. I can make my own way there.'

'Don't be ridiculous,' he replied. 'Have you seen the weather?'

'It's just a bit of rain, I'll be fine.'

'I'll take you,' Dad said firmly. 'You don't want to catch your death of cold before the match on Saturday.'

I sank down on the bed. Why do parents have to be so controlling? Why do they always endeavour to ruin all your plans? Perhaps it's a condition you have to agree to before conception takes place. I couldn't afford to miss Thursday night's practice, so if I didn't take the board down tonight it would have to wait until next week. The phone rang and Dad went to answer it in his bedroom. I grabbed my opportunity and charged downstairs. The kitchen door was open and I could see Mum sitting at the table clutching a mug of tea while helping Emma with her reading homework.

'I'm off,' I said. 'Tell Dad I couldn't wait. I'm taking the bike.'

She waved a hand distractedly. She either hadn't noticed the deluge outside the window or didn't care that I might be washed away in a flash flood. I slipped quickly through to the utility room and closed the door behind me in case her obviously dormant maternal instincts suddenly reactivated themselves.

I started to cycle up the road in the direction of the table-tennis club just in case anyone was watching out of the window. As soon as I was out of sight I doubled back along deserted side streets, pedalling as fast as my legs would go. Every time I heard a car approaching I was convinced it was Dad coming to find me. I just hoped he wouldn't drive all the way to the club and discover I wasn't there.

The main road to Gran and Grandad's was a dual carriageway. I'd never cycled this way before as Mum and Dad said it was too busy. I hate to admit it, but for once they were right. The cars rushed past me like lunatic lemmings and I had to brace myself against the backdraught that tried its best to un-balance me. There was a constant stinging spray from the cars, as well as rain blowing straight into my face. It was miserable. I screwed my eyes up, tucked my head down and pushed hard on the pedals. In the end I pulled onto the pavement, got off the bike and walked.

I hauled myself and the bike up the long hill, past the petrol station and the supermarket and finally turned left into Cherry Tree Avenue. The streetlights aren't so bright here, and the soft orange glow was soothing after the maelstrom of the dual carriageway. I stopped around the corner from Gran and Grandad's house, took the fluorescent armbands off my dripping anorak and stuffed them in my pocket. There was no one about so I pushed the bike into a dense conifer and strolled along the pavement. The only sounds were the hum of distant traffic and the thrumming beat of the raindrops on the ground. My breath, which had come in gasps only a few minutes before, was now even and quiet.

There was a light on in Gran and Grandad's hall, beaming through the stained-glass panel in the centre of the door. The rest of the house was in darkness. I crossed the road, eased open one of the double wooden gates and crouched down on the driveway. The board was attached to one of the gateposts. I put my hands around the rough wooden pole and tugged but it didn't even shiver. Inside my pocket were a pair of Dad's pliers and a torch. I took them out and shuffled closer. A shrub released a shower of water down my back. The torch, which always seemed pathetic when I used it under the duvet for after-hours reading, looked like a searchlight from a high security prison as its beam concentrated on the right spot.

Five long nails held the board in place against the gatepost. Three of them came out really easily as they hadn't been hit home hard. The other two were more troublesome. The pliers were wet and my hands were cold. Neither of them gripped properly. I reached for the hammer that I'd decided to bring at the last moment. Someone walked past on the other side of the road with a dog. I tried to dissolve into the darkness of the bush behind me. The dog veered in my direction, but the man tugged him on. I waited a couple of minutes, listening, grinding my teeth together impatiently.

Eventually I took a deep breath and banged the hammer against the post. The sound seemed to split the air like a thunderclap, but the board moved slightly. I hit it again and again and again, as quickly as I could. The noise made my eardrums hum. I stood up and leaned against the board, pushing it with all my body weight. There was a noise behind me as the front door opened and Gran stepped out onto the porch. I pressed the OFF button on top of the torch and froze. She looked around, peering into the darkness, briefly turning her head in my direction. I was sure she must have seen me, but she just bent down and deposited some empty milk bottles on the step and went back inside.

I let out a long breath, stepped backwards onto the sticky soil, and gave the board a massive tug. Several splinters pierced my palms as the board came away from the gatepost with a crunching sound. I staggered backwards and fell flat on my back in the middle of Grandad's wallflowers with the For Sale board on top of me. I was soaking wet, dirty and freezing cold, but I didn't care. This was the first time I'd done anything vaguely bad and not got caught. The board wasn't as heavy as I had expected and it wasn't too difficult to drag it back to my bike. I balanced it across the handlebars and saddle and started to weave my way through the maze of back roads. This way I reckoned I was less likely to be spotted. Even in my post-vandalistic euphoria I realized that a girl manoeuvring a For Sale board beside a main road in the dark might be a tiny bit suspicious. Every time I saw a car coming or heard footsteps I steered the bike into the shadows.

At last the orange lights of the supermarket sign flaunted themselves in the distance. I bumped the bike down the steps that led to the bottom end of the car park, furthest away from the store itself, and leaned it carefully against the bottle banks. The board clattered to the ground and I trailed it behind the big metal bins, trying my best to hide it under the tangle of urban landscaping, as we call it in geography. Brambles to you and me. By the time I'd finished, the board was mainly out of sight and my hands were covered in scratches to add to the scabs and splinters. Suddenly I felt exhausted. All I wanted was to get home and soak in a hot bubbly bath. Grandad's face flashed into my head. He'd be so angry if he found out what I'd done, but I knew it had to be worth it.

Dad's car was still in the front drive when I got home. I said a silent thank-you for the occasional benefits of mid-week football on television, which must have distracted him from going to collect me. As long as my coach hadn't phoned to find out where I was I should have got away with it. I pushed my bike down the side of the house and fumbled in my pocket for my front-door key.

'Damn!' I hissed, skulking towards the porch. Muffin uncurled from the mat and miaowed at me to let her in. 'You haven't got a key on you, have you, Muffin? I forgot to bring mine.'

I couldn't ring the bell. Mum and Dad would take one look at me and know I'd been up to something. 'If you had a bigger catflap and I had a smaller bum there'd be no problem,' I whispered.

She wound herself around my legs and started to purr. Nick's light flicked on in his bedroom. I grabbed a stone from the drive and threw it. It clinked against the glass and after a couple of seconds Nick's face appeared. I leaped up and down like a maniac, trying to attract his attention. He opened the window.

'What's the matter?' he bellowed.

I put my finger to my mouth. 'Can you let me in, quietly?'

He appeared at the front door in less than a minute, but it seemed like a lifetime. He looked me up and down.

'Has there been a mudquake at the table-tennis club or did you just decide to invent a new sport and sling mud pies at each other instead of little white balls?'

I ignored him and prised my shoes off.

'You can't come in here like that. You're filthy. You'll have to go round to the back.'

I couldn't believe it. 'Have you had a brain transplant while I was out,' I growled, 'or are you Mum disguised as an eleven-year-old nitwit? Anyway, where is she?'

He pointed to the sitting room. I pushed past him and made a dash for the stairs.

'Dad's really annoyed you went off without waiting for him.' He gave me one of his deep, thoughtful looks. 'Kat, where have you been?'

'Just cover for me while I get changed, will you?'

'Kat' – he stalked me up the stairs – 'what have you been up to?'

'Look, Nick, really, it's better that you don't know,' I said and slammed the bathroom door in his face.

CHAPTER 12

Laura was aching to know if I'd gone ahead with the plan. I could tell by the way she glanced at me when I got to school the next morning. Normally on Wednesdays Daniel has her undivided attention, but obviously she'd been half-watching for me and her whole body seethed with curiosity. I sauntered over to a group of girls from my year and tried to pretend Laura wasn't even on the same planet, let alone in the same playground.

There are two ways of ignoring someone. The first way is the proper way and probably the best: you just don't think about them. They don't enter your thought-pattern from one day to the next, and if you do bump into them by mistake you turn away. As soon as they've gone past, they're out of sight and out of mind until the next time you meet. No big deal.

Then there's my way. I pretend to ignore the person, but all the time I'm scanning the street, the classroom, the playground to see where they are. I'm prepared to bump into them at any moment, with a cutting word at the ready, so I'm not taken unawares and left stammering and floundering with embarrassment. I used to be like that with Daniel. My way ensures that you're poised and in control of the situation at all times. The only downside is that the person permanently occupies your subconscious, and although you're trying to ignore them they're actually taking over your whole life. Part of me wanted to tell Laura what I'd done, to see her face widen in amazement with a mixture of admiration and regret that she hadn't helped, but another part of me daren't risk it. The way she was behaving at the moment she'd probably tell me how stupid I was being or, even worse, just laugh.

The next couple of days were a huge anticlimax. Laura had obviously taken a vow of silence as far as I was concerned. She even moved her chair away from me to the farthest edge of her desk. She was almost sitting in the aisle. It was pathetic, but if she felt like that I didn't want to be any nearer to her than I had to be so I moved my chair away too. Mrs Hawk was especially keen on our desks being in parallel lines, but even she didn't comment on the wiggle in the third row from the front. Although I wanted to tell Mum about Laura, it didn't seem fair to burden her with my problems. She'd got enough of her own. Nick didn't ask again about what I'd been up to on Tuesday night, which annoyed me slightly. Don't boys possess a curiosity gene or are they just better at keeping their nosiness under control? Almost worst of all were the sympathy-oozing looks from Mrs

Hawk and a suddenly discovered tolerance for my mathematical bungling. Everyone noticed, and it was embarrassing. I half wished her back to her normal, snarling self.

Mum was unnervingly placid with Dad, which meant everyone started going around in crumpled clothes again and he kept putting his arm around her or stroking the back of her neck as he walked past. No one mentioned the For Sale board and I began to wonder if I'd just dreamed that I'd stolen it. Everything was very odd.

Dad dropped the bombshell on Thursday evening. Table-tennis practice had been a bit of a slog. Grandad still hadn't come along to watch and my coach had bawled me out for Tuesday's absence and not taking things seriously; Laura had never been in a sulk with me for this long before: I was not in a good mood.

'The house has been sold.'

I was getting a yoghurt out of the fridge and I let the cold air permeate my skin while I tried to imagine someone else living in Gran and Grandad's house. It was impossible.

'It can't have been,' I snapped. It was an automatic reaction and as soon as the words left my mouth I knew they shouldn't have. I closed the fridge door slowly, hoping no one would ask why I'd said that.

'Well, it has.' The relief in Dad's voice was

unmistakable. 'Despite some idiot running off with the For Sale board on Tuesday night.'

Nick jutted his chin out and started to chew the end of his pencil. He didn't look at me. He didn't have to. I knew what he was thinking. I felt myself flushing and wondered if I should root around in the fridge again to stop my face resembling a ripe tomato.

'Luckily these buyers had looked round on Sunday, then went back again yesterday and made an offer of the asking price. Gran and Grandad have accepted it.'

I looked at Mum. Her nose was turning pink at the end and her eyelids flitted up and down over glistening eyeballs.

'The new people have sold their own house and are living in rented accommodation so they're keen to move in as quickly as possible,' Dad carried on, resting a hand on Mum's shoulder. 'It's for the best that it's happening quickly.'

Mum lifted her arm and intertwined her fingers with Dad's. They were traitors. I felt disgusted.

'How can you say that?' I yelled. 'It's as if you can't wait to get rid of him. What have you done to try and persuade him to stay? Nothing.'

Mum started to sob. Nick stared down at his maths homework and Emma sidled across the kitchen to clutch at Dad's sleeve.

'What have any of you done to stop him going?' I

glared at all of them. 'Sometimes I think I'm the only one that cares.'

They stared back, angry, reproachful, hurt. The space which lay between us across the kitchen floor felt like no man's land. I flounced out, slamming the door with a force Mum would have been proud of. She could get a first-class degree with honours in door-slamming. First you toss your head back. It's better if you have long, silky hair like Em. The wiry stuff like mine and Mum's doesn't have quite the same petulant swing to it. Then you stomp out. It's important at this point not to trip over the edge of the carpet and fall flat on your face or fumble with the door handle. Once the handle came off in my hand and I couldn't even open the door, let alone slam it. I knew then why Mum got so annoyed with Dad for never completing all those DIY jobs around the house. The slamming is really the chocolate on the profiterole. Some doors are slammers and some aren't. Fortunately for Mum and me, ours are. As I stamped upstairs I could still sense the walls vibrating and the mortar turning to powder between the bricks. I wondered how much door-slamming it takes to make a house fall down.

I lay on my bed and tried to lick the yoghurt out of the carton with my tongue. I couldn't believe it. All that effort, splinters in my already wounded palms, the dangers of hypothermia, the risk of being grounded for years if I was caught – and it had been for nothing. I could hear them downstairs, opening cupboards, Nick scraping his chair back on the kitchen floor, everyone carrying on as normal, leaving me to fester. It was an hour before anyone tapped on my door. I expected it to be Dad the Conciliator, but it was Nick who warily peeped into the room.

'Are you OK?'

'Of course.' I tried to sound convincing, as much for myself as anything.

He ventured in a bit further, like a boy entering a lion's cage. I lay on my bed and watched him as he prowled around, picking things up and putting them down again in exactly the same place.

'It was you, wasn't it? You took the board down.'

I nodded. His mouth dropped open.

'That's really cool, Kat. I'd have come and helped if you'd told me.'

'Could I have helped too?' Emma stood in the doorway in her pyjamas.

I leaped off the bed and dragged her into my room.

'Did you steal the board?' she asked.

'I just borrowed it, Emma. I wanted to give us a bit more time to try and change Grandad's mind. You mustn't tell anyone I took it. OK?'

She nodded.

'It's our secret' – I glanced at Nick – 'the three of us.'

They both nodded.

'I'm sorry it didn't work,' Nick mumbled.

'Don't worry.' I didn't sound as bright as I'd hoped. 'I've got another plan up my sleeve.'

Emma and Nick looked doubtful.

'I can't tell you what it is, but don't worry. It isn't anything bad.'

I smiled, but inside my stomach heaved. This plan was a last resort, a real sacrifice. If this didn't work, nothing would.

CHAPTER 13

Laura apologized first. She passed me a note during English. It just said 'Sorry'. I tore a bit of paper out of my rough book, wrote on it 'Me too' and passed it over to her. She sort of smiled and carried on writing her essay. We sidled up to each other at break and squatted down on the steps to the art room. We didn't talk about anything personal, just stuck to school stuff. It seemed safer, especially as I was eating an apple and we were both aware that it could be a lethal missile at short range!

'Good luck with the match tomorrow,' she said as we walked out of the gates at the end of the afternoon. Her mum was already waiting in the car, tapping her fingers impatiently against the steering wheel.

'Thanks,' I murmured. 'I'm going to need it.' That was what I always said before a match and Laura always responded in the same way.

'You'll be fine,' she said, but this time she didn't touch my arm or give me a hug like she used to. 'You're bound to win as long as you're playing for the right reason.'

'What do you mean?'

She kicked at a loose bit of gravel. 'Look, Kat' – there was an impatient edge to her voice – 'you'll be fine as long as you're playing because it's what *you* want and . . .'

'And what?' My voice was tetchy too.

'You've got to want to win for yourself and not for someone else.'

I watched as she slid into the passenger seat and mouthed 'Good luck' out of the window as the car pulled away into the traffic. I knew she was right, but winning wasn't the important thing any more – it was losing that mattered.

I sensed someone hovering behind me and I swung round, flicking my scarf over one shoulder. Daniel half smiled and shifted uneasily from one foot to the other. I felt flustered and hot. I knew I looked a complete mess and hid my ink-splodged hands behind my back.

'Have you two made up then?' His eyebrows slunk together as he frowned at the retreating car.

I nodded and started to walk. He didn't fall into step beside me but I could feel his eyes following me as I stomped towards the corner. I felt strangely disappointed that he hadn't followed, but put it down to my hormones. Mum says they're responsible for all sorts of irrational behaviour.

'Katrina?' Suddenly he was there, striding next to me, and I jumped.

'You nearly gave me a heart attack!'

'Sorry.'

'Hasn't anyone ever told you not to creep up on people?'

'Sorry,' he said again. 'I wasn't really creeping. It's a bit difficult with size twelve feet.'

'Well, it felt distinctly like creeping to me,' I snapped. My heart was hammering against my ribs and I knew it wasn't just because he'd startled me.

'So—'

'Don't say sorry again,' I interrupted.

We looked at each other and burst out laughing. His eyes crinkled up at the corners and a dimple appeared in one cheek. I look like a constipated cat when I laugh, but he didn't turn away in disgust. Feelings are weird. They're a bit like parents – maddeningly inconsistent. You think you know where you are with them and suddenly they behave totally unpredictably. Somehow, somewhere, my feelings for Daniel had changed. Looking back, I could see it had happened gradually, but at the time I blocked it off, didn't want to admit it to myself, didn't want any more complications in my life.

'I'm glad you and Laura are friends again,' he said, 'because I wanted to ask you a favour.'

That was when I knew for sure that his feelings for me had changed too. I bit my lip to hide my confusion. I felt like he looked, awkward and self-conscious. It felt as if we'd only just met, not known each other for years.

'Can we stop for a minute?'

I perched on the edge of a low garden wall and he sat down next to me, dropping his bag between his feet. His knees splayed outwards and I shifted along slightly so there was no danger of us touching. Even at the end of the school day he smelled nice, a musky mixture of soap and hair gel and leather from his jacket. I hoped I wasn't assaulting him with onion breath from my lunch-time crisps or emitting the ponging perfume of the gym after a gruelling session on the ropes.

'We're moving away.' He cracked his knuckles. 'My dad's been offered a job in Yorkshire.'

If he'd told me a few weeks previously I'd have been pleased, relieved, but now I was horrified. It felt as if my stomach had bungee-jumped down to my ankles and back up into my throat. First Grandad, now Daniel. I knew my voice would sound croaky so I didn't try to speak.

'Laura doesn't know yet.'

Poor Laura. If *I* felt bad, how on earth would she take the news? 'She'll be really upset.' I whispered.

'Will you keep an eye on her for me? Make sure she's OK and doesn't get into any trouble?'

'Laura – in trouble?' I tried to sound light-hearted. 'The teachers' ideal pupil? You must be joking!'

He didn't smile. 'Do you remember when our parents split up, how she withdrew from everything for a while, dropped out of the choir, didn't bother in lessons or hand in her homework? The only person she didn't shut out was you. As long as she's got you to rely on I won't worry so much.'

'Of course she has,' I murmured.

He fiddled with his rucksack strap as if he was about to go, but he didn't. He just sat there looking thoroughly miserable.

'Do you mind going away?'

His chin dropped lower so it was almost touching his chest. It was obviously a stupid question, but those are the ones that tend to get blurted out at difficult moments.

'Dad says jobs like this don't come along very often. He says it's a good opportunity to make a fresh start.'

I wanted to put my hand over his but I didn't dare. We just sat next to each other for a while, thinking, wishing, hoping.

'We'd better get home.' He stood up abruptly. 'It'll be dark soon.'

'It's always dark these days,' I answered softly.

His fingers brushed against mine and a hundred tiny sparks fizzed up my arm.

'Laura's lucky to have a friend like you, Katrina.'

I pulled my scarf further up towards my face and blushed. I longed to say I was his friend too, that he could rely on me, but I chickened out and hoped he knew it anyway.

We separated at the traffic lights. He grabbed my arm as I was about to cross the road.

'Don't say anything to Laura, just yet.' His fingers were light but firm as they held my coat.

'Course not.' He relaxed his grip and I bolted across as the green man started to flash.

'Good luck with the match tomorrow,' he called.

'Thanks,' I replied, surprised he knew about it, but he was already walking away and my voice was lost in the roar of the Friday afternoon rush hour.

Saturday was when my last-resort plan to keep Grandad in this country had to be put into action. The most important thing was to behave absolutely normally so as not to arouse any suspicion. For once I didn't feel nervous about the match. When you *plan* to lose there's not a lot to get jittery about.

'Big day tomorrow,' Dad said as he hacked off the burnt bits at the bottom of a saucepan. Mum had decided the best thing for me prior to my game was a good dose of home-prepared charcoal. It was definitely time she went back to work.

'Now there's nothing to worry about,' Mum said. 'You'll be fine.'

'Mmm,' I answered, trying to look anxious and obviously not succeeding.

'You seem very calm, for once,' Nick remarked.

'Oh, not really,' I protested. 'Inside here' – I tapped my tummy – 'it's like a raging, swelling storm.'

'It's the nerves, darling.' Mum stroked my hair and snagged a well-bitten nail in one of my curls. 'But you're like me, you hide them well.'

Nick shook his head in disbelief.

'What you need is an early night,' said Mum.

For once I agreed, and straight after supper escaped to the safety of my room.

CHAPTER 14

I'd played Cathy Hazelwood several times before and we were pretty even in terms of winning. I knew it was difficult to beat her but it had never occurred to me that I'd have trouble losing. It was amazing how easy it had been to take the decision to throw the match. For years I'd been working my way up the rankings, yet suddenly table tennis seemed so trivial. Losing was my last chance to persuade Grandad to stay, and nothing else mattered as much as that. I'd planned my strategy. At the beginning I'd play my best to avoid raising any suspicions; then about halfway through I'd start making a few mistakes. Cathy would go in for the kill at the first sign of weakness and it would all be over painlessly and quickly. It seemed foolproof.

Dad and Nick said they were coming to give me moral support. For once I didn't argue. I could always claim they had made me more nervous and contributed to me losing. It would be rather unfair to heap the blame onto them, but it was in a good cause.

'Is Grandad coming?' I'd asked Dad as he drove to

the club. Nick sat in the back seat, mesmerized by the sound from his personal stereo.

'Perhaps.'

'I need him there. I can't win without him.'

Dad shrugged his shoulders. 'I can't make him come if he doesn't want to.'

That hurt and he knew it but he didn't apologize. He pinched my cheek lightly. 'Anyway, don't be silly. Of course you can win without him there.'

'No!' I raised my voice and saw Dad's startled glance, sensed Nick divert his attention towards me. 'You don't understand,' I shouted. 'I need him to watch me. He's like my lucky mascot.'

Grandad *did* turn up just before the start of the match. He gave a cheerful wave and sat down next to Dad. It was the first time he'd been to watch me for ages and I wondered if he was having second thoughts about going to Spain. I pretended to kiss my bat for luck, but I was careful not to let my lips touch the rubber.

The game went badly from the start. Cathy seemed as nervous as I would have been if *I'd* been playing to win. She hit her returns of serve into the net and played too many long balls. Soon I'd taken a seven-point lead and knew she'd have trouble catching up if she didn't raise her game or I didn't lower mine to toddler level. She was getting really narked with herself, and the worse I tried to play to help her out, the worse her game got. I caught Grandad's eye and quickly looked away. His face was set as solid as one of Mum's coffee mousses. He looked really angry. It was almost as if he knew what I was trying to do.

Suddenly Cathy seemed to pull herself together and the gap in our scores started to narrow. I let out a small sigh. For an awful moment I'd thought she was going to let me win. She hit a spectacular forehand drive and it was nineteen points apiece. I only had to let her have the next two points and it would all be over.

I did a quick rehearsal in my head, pretending to be distraught, and imagined the change of expression on Grandad's face as he comforted me and said he'd have to stay after all, as I obviously needed his help more than he'd realized. I thought how it would give him a sense of purpose again and allowed myself a smug smile. Cathy caressed the ball as she waited to serve. Her relief that she hadn't been totally humiliated glittered in her eyes.

I turned away for a moment, pretending to adjust my hair clips, as Grandad's constant advice echoed inside my head – 'As long as you do your best,' he said, 'then you can hold your head up and be proud of yourself.' I couldn't remember a match when I hadn't followed that advice, even when I was feeling ill or tired. Sometimes I'd lost, but it hadn't seemed so bad because I'd put the maximum effort into the game.

I took a deep breath and turned back to the table.

Cathy scowled at me for the delay and then I saw that look on her face that I'd seen several times before. She was poised for the kill. She thought I was beaten, that she had won.

'As long as you're doing it because it's what *you* want' – Laura's words battered Grandad's out of the way as the ball came spinning towards me. Who have I been playing for all these years? I asked myself. For a few seconds I wasn't sure. I slammed the ball back across the net, trying to suppress the feeling that was spreading through every cell in my body. It was a hopeless fight. My cool resolve to lose with dignity withered, and as I stared across the dark green table I could not, would not, allow Cathy Hazelwood to win without a fight.

All the spectators became a blur, along with the consequences of what I was about to do. Cathy raised a perfectly arched eyebrow as she was beaten by the viciousness of my return, and I clenched my fingers tightly around my bat handle in satisfaction. From then on I was totally focused on that small white ball and the familiar desire to win. The final score was 25–23 to me.

As we shook hands Cathy looked devastated and I knew just how she felt. The euphoria I'd felt as the winning shot zipped past her and I heard Nick's triumphal shout dissolved instantly. She looked as if she was about to cry. I felt like joining her.

'What have I done?' I whispered to myself as I

zipped up my tracksuit top. 'What have I done?' I couldn't believe it. I'd just ruined my last hope of getting Grandad to stay.

My coach ambled over. 'Not exactly a glorious victory.' I looked suitably embarrassed. 'You were lucky to get away with that. I'll put it down to the fact you weren't well on Tuesday.'

Dad's eyes widened and I changed the subject quickly.

'Where's Grandad?' I scanned the room.

'He had to go,' Dad replied. 'He's got a few things to do.'

I found out what Grandad had to do when we went round for tea later. I thought it was a bit odd when Mum and Dad said they were coming too.

'What, and miss the opportunity of coming home and having a good row?' I whispered to Nick as we waited for Dad to get the car out of the garage. 'Things must be serious.'

'Actually they haven't been rowing so much recently, or haven't you noticed?'

I realized he was right. Things had been calmer in the parental strife department. The atmosphere in our house was not exactly tranquil, but there seemed to be a truce on the verbal warfare and I hadn't noticed any airborne domestic items flying in Dad's direction for a little while. I suppose there'd been so much else going on I hadn't taken it in.

'I thought you were going to lose that game on purpose.' Nick bit the end of his thumb.

I gave him a sideways stare. 'Can't you recognize stunning tactics when you see them?'

He pulled a face. 'Are you sure you didn't think Grandad would stay to help out with the coaching if you lost?'

I paused before answering. 'Are you really my brother or are you some alien life form with strange telepathic qualities?'

He grinned. 'I was right then?'

'You're not as stupid as you look, are you?'

'Unlike some people,' he shot back. 'It wouldn't have worked, you know. It was a pathetic idea.'

I shrugged and zipped my anorak right up to the top so it hid my mouth. 'I couldn't do it in the end,' I said in a muffled voice. 'The thing is, Nick, when it came to those last few points I just had to try my best, had to at least try and win. That doesn't mean that table tennis is more important than Grandad.'

'God, Kat' – he glared at me – 'don't you think I know that?'

I felt small and stupid and naïve. Suddenly I realized that Nick understood me almost better than I knew myself. It made me feel disconcerted and comforted at the same time. Illogically I wondered if Mum and Dad had got mixed up because we were quite close together in age. Perhaps it was Nick who was the eldest child, not me.

Mum's huge green trunk that she used to take to boarding school was parked in Gran and Grandad's hall. Next to it was a pile of things carelessly wrapped in newspaper. Everyone except Emma pretended they hadn't seen anything unusual. Perma-frost seemed to have replaced the marrow in my bones.

'What's this doing here?' Emma asked.

Grandad appeared at the top of the stairs. 'I'm putting a few things in it, Emma love.' He leaned heavily on the banister rail as he came down, a couple of large books snuggled under his free arm.

'To take to Spain?' she asked, stepping into the trunk. I wanted to go and haul her out, but we all seemed rooted to the spot except for Emma and Grandad. She lay down, scrunching her knees up and folding her arms across her chest. 'You could take me with you, Grandad,' she giggled.

He bent over and started to tickle her under her chin the same way he used to with Nick and me. I closed my eyes, wished I could close my ears so I couldn't hear Emma's giggles and Grandad's chuckling.

'You don't need to start packing yet, do you?' It was my voice but I hadn't planned to say anything.

Grandad straightened up and Gran bolted into the kitchen. Mum followed her and I heard them clattering cups and saucers onto the tray. Another secret hovered in the hall air along with the lavender-scented furniture polish. I put my hand across my mouth and waited.

'I'm flying out early next week.' Grandad didn't look at any of us. He seemed to be studying the pattern on the hall rug. Emma lay uncharacteristically quiet in the bottom of the trunk. 'We've got buyers for the house, the weather here is lousy and I can live very cheaply in a Spanish hotel at this time of year. It'll give me time to look around for the right house.'

I think I'd really known right from the beginning that Grandad would go whatever I did, but it didn't make this moment any easier. I'd still deluded myself with a few morsels of hope. Stupid really. Nick started to sniff and Dad pulled him close.

'So that's why you came to watch me today,' I whispered. 'Because it was the last time.'

Grandad took a few paces forward and stopped. He must have sensed I wouldn't let him touch me, that any physical show of affection seemed hugely hypocritical. He cleared his throat.

'You don't need me there to help you win.'

He was right and I'd known it for ages, but I wouldn't admit it. Especially not to him. Not yet. Why should I let him off the hook so easily?

'Well, you won't know that in future, will you?' I spat out the words. 'Because you won't be here to find out.'

He shook his head. 'Katy, I'm so—'

'Don't, don't, don't!' I screamed. 'Don't you dare say you're sorry.'

I stormed into the dining room and sat at the large rectangular table where we all used to gather for Christmas dinner. I sat there while Mum, Dad and Gran drank tea in the kitchen and Nick dismantled the train set and Emma helped Grandad wrap more things to put in the trunk. I sat there until it was dark and I couldn't see the telltale patches of wallpaper where Grandad had removed pictures, or the spaces on the mantelpiece where he'd taken a few pieces of heirloom silver. I sat there until it was so dark I could pretend everything was back in its proper place, just as it used to be.

CHAPTER 15

Sunday was dismal. Laura didn't phone to see how the match had gone, so I didn't bother to contact her. Nobody seemed to feel like talking. Mum decided to tidy the kitchen cupboards and found various bottles and packets that were about a hundred years past their sell-by date, but she wouldn't throw them out. It was probably part of some long-term plot to poison Dad when she tired of all the arguing.

Dad disappeared into the garden to sow some grass seed on the threadbare lawn. It was obviously going to be washed away in the biblical deluge that had been pouring down since breakfast. Even I could calculate it would be swilled down the hill, onto the patio and into the gaps between the crazy paving that Dad had never got around to cementing. This would definitely be grounds for divorce in the spring when the seed germinated, and I wondered whether to say anything in my marriage guidance capacity but decided against it.

Nick actually volunteered to do his piano practice and played the most morose piece of music he could find over and over again. Even Emma seemed affected by the gloom. She sat at the kitchen table drawing seriously weird pictures of witches and wizards. I made a cake. It wasn't anything fancy, just a plain Victoria sponge, but it rose beautifully. I filled it with some of Gran's home-made raspberry jam, dusted the top with icing sugar and cut the first slice for myself while the sponge was still slightly warm. I looked at the cake with one slice missing and thought that in a few days our family would be like that.

Laura looked terrible on Monday morning. There were bruising shadows under her eyes that toned in with the slight blueness around her mouth. She hugged herself fiercely.

'You OK?' I asked.

'Fine.' She looked straight over my shoulder. Her hostility formed a force field between us.

'Good weekend?' I asked.

'Fine.'

I pressed my fingers against my lips. Laura was obviously in need of a major cheering-up session and I could guess why. The trouble was, I wasn't in the mood. Besides, anyone who so much as looked at my down-in-the-dumps expression would probably feel like stepping out in front of a bus. Laura's stepdad had obviously told her what I wasn't meant to know, so I couldn't say anything until she did.

'I won the table tennis.'

'Good.'

'Laura, there's obviously something wrong. What is it?'

She rounded on me so unexpectedly I staggered backwards into several other kids. They shouted belligerently.

'*You're* what's wrong, Kat,' she hissed. 'I thought you were my friend. I thought we didn't have any secrets from each other.'

There was no point pretending any more. 'Daniel asked me not to say anything,' I stammered. 'What could I do?'

Laura's pale cheeks suddenly flared pink and she raised her voice. 'That's right – blame Daniel.'

'We were only thinking of you, trying to protect you,' I said lamely. Mum and Dad's words spilled out of my mouth and I despised myself.

'That's no excuse,' she whispered, but she didn't sound too convinced by her own reply.

I thought it was a pretty good reason not to tell her. Hadn't it meant she'd been happy in her ignorance for longer? Wouldn't it have been better for me if I hadn't found out about Grandad when I did? She was close to tears and fumbled in her pocket for a tissue.

'Look, Laura, it's Yorkshire, not the other side of the world.' I was tempted to add, It's not Spain, but even I'm not that insensitive. 'You'll be able to go and visit every weekend and stuff yourself with cakes in Betty's tea rooms.'

'I'll get fat,' she answered. She didn't sound quite so angry. I was encouraged to carry on.

'Nah, you'll walk it all off on long treks across the moors before navigating your way to Harvey Nicks. Your dad will feel so guilty about separating you and Daniel he'll buy you anything you want. Now is the time to be really mercenary and ask for that mega-expensive suede coat you want.'

She half smiled.

'You may be traumatized,' I carried on as lightly as I could; 'you will probably have an acne eruption that dermatologists would rave over *and* blisters the size of a national park, but you'll have a wardrobe to die for.'

The bell went for first lesson and I was already exhausted.

'You should have told me,' she said as we walked across the yard, and although her iciness had thawed, I knew that I wasn't totally forgiven. I also knew that I didn't deserve to be.

Grandad was due to leave the following morning. His taxi was arriving early to take him to the airport, so we all went to say goodbye on the Monday evening. Gran made copious cups of tea to lubricate the stilted conversation. I sat in a corner and watched everyone. Gran reminded me of those newly planted trees you see at the side of the motorway, fragile and vulnerable. She looked as if she needed something to support her, as if one more angry word would snap her in two. Mum sat on the sofa, struggling silently to conceal the anger that had overtaken her grief-stricken sobbing, but it was touch and go whether she'd be able to restrain herself from saying something. She didn't usually manage it.

Nick was quiet and grown-up and civilized. He behaved in a way everyone else probably envied. I was really proud of him. Dad didn't manage quite as well as Nick. His mouth looked as if it'd been sewn up too tightly at the corners and his sentences were a bit on the brusque side. Emma sat quietly on Grandad's knee, picking the chocolate chips out of her biscuit and popping them into his mouth. It was heart-breaking to watch. Grandad, on the other hand, fizzed with poorly suppressed excitement. He obviously couldn't wait to get on that plane and start his new life, and I hated him for it.

'I suppose it's rather an adventure for your grandad,' Mrs Hawk had said to me the previous week.

I looked up in amazement. I'd stayed in at break time to grapple with some tricky fractions. Mrs Hawk said it would only take a few minutes for me to get to grips with them. I hadn't mentioned Grandad at all. *He's my grandad*, I felt like saying to her, *not James Bond or Indiana Jones. He should have stopped having adventures forty years ago.* Instead I kept quiet, my eyes fixed firmly on the page in front of me.

'Quite a challenge,' she murmured admiringly.

I knew she didn't mean the fractions. That did it. I plonked my pencil down and looked straight into her eyes.

'He's had a stroke,' I said firmly; 'he's had to learn to talk, walk and write again. Surely that's been enough of a challenge for him without swanning off to Spain on a whim?'

She twitched nervously and fingered a dangly earring in the shape of a turtle. 'Perhaps it's not a whim,' she replied slowly. 'Perhaps he's always had this dream.'

'He hasn't. I'd have known about it.'

She looked at me and smiled. It was one of those really irritating, condescending smiles that adults do so well, implying with just a few minor muscle movements that they think they know so much and we know so little.

'Sometimes you get to a stage in life where it's now or never, when you know that you've just got to try something different, whatever the consequences.'

She'd gone all misty eyed and dreamily distant. I shuffled in my seat, sensing that we were on dangerous ground; that this conversation was not just to do with Grandad and me.

'I think your grandad is an inspiration.'

I stared at her in amazement. How on earth could she make a statement like that when she'd never even met Grandad? *You couldn't be more wrong*, I wanted to shout. Grandad isn't inspiring. He's behaving like a spoilt child who's not willing to compromise. He wants to have it all his own way and do just what he wants without a thought for anyone else.

Now, as we moved through to the hall and said our goodbyes and everyone fought back the tears, a tiny bit of me admitted that Mrs Hawk was right in one way. Grandad was brave to be going abroad, totally alone, not knowing anyone when he got there, with the possibility looming over him that he could be taken ill again at any time. I also thought he was very stupid.

'You can come and visit,' Grandad said to Emma, 'and there's always the telephone.' He threw his good arm around Nick's steeled shoulders. Nick bit his lip so hard I thought he'd draw blood.

'And you'll come back to visit us, won't you, Grandad?' Emma clung to his hand.

He nodded, but I knew he was lying to her. He wouldn't come back, not for ages – perhaps not ever. He was in too much of a hurry to go to consider things like that.

'Take care,' Dad said and Grandad patted him on the back.

Mum hovered by the front door, the telltale snail trails of wiped-away tears shimmering down her face. I moved over and took her hand. She squeezed my fingers and half-leaned on me.

Grandad came over and put his hands on my

shoulders. I looked at his perfectly polished brown lace-up shoes and thought how hot his feet would get in Spain if he wore those. I knew if I concentrated hard on practical thoughts I could dam the torrent of tears that was battering my insides, making my head throb and my throat feel as if it was closing up.

'Keep going with that table tennis,' he murmured. 'Don't want you getting distracted by boys and discos.' He leaned forward and hugged me.

I breathed in his aftershave, the tweediness of his jacket, and tried to preserve it in some safe corner of my brain. It was a brief hug and our bodies barely touched. It was for the best. Anything more would have crucified me. Mum stiffened beside me as he kissed her gingerly on the cheek, as if afraid she'd turn away. She didn't, but her injured expression must have stopped him showing more emotion.

'I'll miss you,' she choked.

He blinked and shied away, seeming to melt slightly in the gloom of the hall. It was cruel not to say that he'd miss us too, but then he'd never been good at the 'I love you's even before the stroke. Back then he'd shown his love for us with time and patience and an unquenchable interest in what we were doing. It had seemed enough. We hadn't needed words. We did now. Nothing else would do, but he couldn't say them. He couldn't find the courage to say what he knew we all wanted to hear. Perhaps he thought talk of love would weaken his resolve to go, or perhaps he didn't love us as much any more. Perhaps the stroke had changed him, turned him into someone totally different, and we were so busy trying to get him better, trying to get the old Grandad back, that we hadn't noticed.

I wanted to believe that theory so much, but deep down I wasn't sure it was the right one. Tapping away at the back of my head was another thought – that Grandad had always been a bit detached, that this side of his character was always there, lurking in the shadows, and I'd loved him too much to notice. The awful, awful thing that I couldn't get out of my head was that Grandad had never really loved me as much as I'd thought.

It was such a relief to scramble into Dad's car, to huddle up in the back, with me in the middle and Em and Nick on either side, to feel safe. Grandad stood on the porch as we pulled away, not waving, just watching with an inscrutable expression. As we turned the corner at the end of the road I twisted round in my seat and looked back. He was still there, standing on the terrazzo step, eyes gazing at the back of the car, and I knew that we might never ever see each other again. Nobody spoke all the way home.

CHAPTER 16

Just when I thought things couldn't get any worse, they did.

The day Grandad left was always bound to be difficult. Everyone's feelings were inevitably going to be as fragile as a home-made meringue. Mum and Dad decreed that everything should carry on as normal, and even an event as momentous as Grandad's leaving didn't warrant a day off school. It was a unanimous parental decision, which was something of a novelty and twice as hard to argue against, so Nick, Em and I just had to go along with it.

The day started with the normal storm in a cereal bowl about some selfish person (me) taking the last helping of chocolate krispies without asking if anyone else wanted it, and the usual complaints from Dad about the eardrum-splitting level of noise from Nick's radio, and everyone shouting at Em because she wouldn't get dressed. It was going to be one of those life-is-falling-apart days, whatever happened, but adults seem convinced that keeping up the same old routine will dull the pain.

Given a choice, I'd have stayed in bed all day and played my most depressing CDs. That way you could make yourself feel even more miserable, which was positive in a way because it meant you hadn't been as depressed as you'd originally thought, after all. I'd half hoped for a Siberian blizzard or a fog as thick as condensed milk to ground all the planes in the country. Any ultra-excessive weather conditions would have done. I wasn't fussy. On the other hand, I knew that would just be delaying the inevitable, so I was sort of relieved to be greeted by pearly pink sky and a warm springlike breeze as Mum half pushed me out of the front door for school.

I checked my watch. Grandad would already be at the airport and soon he'd be up there amongst the candyfloss clouds, travelling to his new life. Sometimes I wished he'd died when he had the stroke. I thought that would have been easier to cope with than this – the fact that he was choosing to leave us. I knew it was a wicked thought that I would never dare to share, and I hated myself for thinking it, hated every microscopic cell in my body, but I couldn't stop it. Sometimes it just forced its way into my head and demanded recognition. I closed my eyes and shook my whole body.

'Go away!' I growled. 'Why can't you just leave me alone?'

'I only wanted to say well done for winning the table tennis.'

I swivelled round. Daniel was just behind me. How could someone so tall walk so softly? I felt my cheeks turning into mini hotplates and my insides did a good impersonation of a dodgy trampoline.

'I didn't mean . . .'

'You needn't bother to explain,' he muttered. He ducked his head, but not before I'd spotted the injured look in his eyes.

'But I do . . .'

He'd already marched past, his long legs striding out as if he couldn't get away from me fast enough.

'Daniel,' I called, 'listen to me . . .' but he was almost out of earshot. If he did hear me he didn't slow down or turn round. I stood watching him galloping into the distance before looking up at the sky.

'Damn you, Grandad,' I said. 'Damn, damn, damn.'

I couldn't concentrate on anything all day. I got my French books out in science, answered totally the wrong question in history and splodged ink all over my blouse in English.

'You could enter that for the Turner Prize,' Laura joked. ' "Ink-comprehensible" would be an appropriate title.'

It was clever, and another day I'd have joined in with the joke, but not today. I was pretty sure Laura hadn't forgotten the date that Grandad was leaving, and when I spotted a plane flying over the playground during break she did put her arm around me briefly. But she didn't say anything. She nudged me with her elbow in music when it was my turn to torture everyone with a tune on the recorder, and she prodded me with her perspex ruler during science when she thought I might be in danger of receiving the teacher's attention. What I really wanted was for her to say something sympathetic. Perhaps she thought it was safer not to; that one kind word could demolish my composure and lead to unrestrained tears. She was probably right. It would have been embarrassing for everyone. Perhaps, like Nick, she knew me better than I realized.

When I got home Dad's car was already in the drive and there was a suitcase in the hall. I could tell by its bulging sides that the case wasn't packed for an overnight stay. My imagination immediately went into overdrive and started to sprint towards the end of our family life.

Nick poked his head round the kitchen door. 'Oh,' he said ominously, 'you're back.'

'Yes,' I answered, 'this is me, in the flesh, returned from a gruelling day being educated. Why's Dad home so early and what's with the suitcase?'

'It's Gran's.'

I swallowed hard with relief but Nick still looked wary.

'What's it doing here?'

'She didn't want to stay in the house on her own so she's come here for a few days.'

'But we haven't got a spare room.' As the words came out of my mouth I saw Nick's eyes widen and followed his darting gaze towards the landing.

'Oh no!' I dropped my rucksack, bounded up the stairs two at a time and pushed open the door to my bedroom – except it wasn't my bedroom any more. It was excruciatingly tidy, a pink bedspread took the place of my dolphin-covered duvet, and my desk and hi-fi were absent without permission. A navy-blue vanity case sat on the dressing table and Gran's bag for her tapestry hung over the back of my chair.

'Katy!' Dad stood behind me and draped his arms over my shoulders. 'I'm sorry this is a bit unexpected, but you've got the biggest room and since it was only decorated last year it looks the nicest.'

'Where am I going to sleep?' It wasn't my most petulant voice, but any teenager would have been pleased with it.

'You'll have to share with Em.'

'How long for? Days? Weeks? Months? Years? Decades . . . ?'

Dad rotated me, his arms still linked, and kissed my creased forehead. 'Don't be awkward, Katy, please.'

I looked pleadingly up into his face. 'Why can't she go into the nursing home with Great-Grandma?'

'Don't be ridiculous.' He sounded exhausted.

'Gran's not *that* old. She just needs a bit of TLC for now. I'm sure she won't be here for long.'

'What if Gran doesn't want to find a new house? What if she decides she doesn't want to live on her own? What if she wants to stay with us for ever? What if she wants my room for ever?'

'Well,' Dad said, 'if that happens, we'll have to deal with it.'

I gasped and wriggled out of his clasp. 'No, Dad! You're not meant to say that. You're meant to re-assure me that it won't be for long, that I'll have my room back soon. And while we're talking about proper parenting, you should have mentioned this to me before, not just dumped it on me at the end of a difficult day.'

'There wasn't time to discuss it,' Dad sighed.

I flounced across the room and stared out of the bay window. 'I'm at a very sensitive age, I need my own space. On top of everything else, this sort of thing could damage me.'

It was a stupid attitude to take. There was an ominous quality in the air like that brief, weird still-ness you get just before a thunderstorm.

'For goodness' sake!' he exploded. 'Don't you think about anyone apart from yourself?'

I was shocked by his tone. Dad's anger is normally an internal force, not profound ranting and raging. That's Mum's territory, but she seemed to have lost her prickliness lately. Perhaps Dad thought it was his turn to take on the mantle of the punishing parent.

'Well if I don't think about me, no one else will.' I knew it sounded martyrish and I was making things worse, but I just couldn't stop myself.

Dad went ballistic. I had never seen him so angry or heard him shout so loudly. 'Don't be so ridiculous. We spend our whole time worrying about you children.'

'Well I worry too,' I shouted back. 'How do I know that you won't go and abandon us the way Grandad has left Mum?'

'I don't know how you can even think that.' He had turned quite pale. 'I would never leave you.'

'But can I be sure of that, Dad? Tell me how I can be sure after everything that's happened. Besides, you couldn't wait for Grandad to go. The sooner the better, you said. Don't you think he didn't know what you thought?'

I waited for him to come and put his arms around me again, to comfort me, to make promises that we both knew might be broken but would make me feel better anyway. I wanted him to treat me like a little girl again and he didn't. He stood quite still and he didn't give me an answer because we were both grown up enough to know there wasn't one that would do. I respected him for it, but I did wish he'd seen the small person standing in front of him and not the tall gangly teenager who looked ten years older than she felt. He turned to leave the room looking shaken.

'I can't cope with this now, Katrina. It's been a terrible day for all of us' – he looked close to tears – 'especially for Gran and Mum, so you've got to try and get a grip on yourself. We all need to pull together. Do you hear me?'

I gave the tiniest nod. Suddenly I wanted to go and throw my arms around him, to say I was sorry, to make him feel better, but I wasn't sure how he'd react so I stayed where I was.

'And don't tell Emma you don't want to share with her. She's thrilled. She's even said you can have the top bunk.'

'Sorry,' I whispered as he turned to leave.

He paused, stood with his back to me, his shoulders slumped, arms hanging loosely by his sides. He looked old.

'I didn't want Grandad to go. You know that.' He didn't turn round. 'He's a stubborn man, a proud man. He may have had a stroke but he can still make his own decisions. He made his mind up to leave a long time ago and I realized that nothing and no one was going to change it, not even you. What was the point in prolonging the pain?'

I listened to Dad's heavy, slow footsteps on the stair carpet and dug my nails into my palms until they left deep red dash marks. He went into the kitchen and slammed the door hard behind him. It was an eight out of ten as slammings go, but it was pretty good for a first attempt. I sank onto the

Aegean-blue carpet and started to cry. I cried so many tears that if that carpet had really been the Aegean, every single Greek island would probably have been totally submerged.

CHAPTER 17

Em woke me up the next morning, banging under the top bunk.

'Kat, wake up! You've got a surprise.'

'What?' I groaned, thinking that nothing would ever surprise me again.

'I think it's a Valentine card.' She climbed the ladder and waved a rhubarb-coloured envelope in front of me.

I slid my finger under the flap and ripped it open. In the past Grandad had sent me the occasional Valentine, but his cards were normally cute and cuddly with sweet-talking rhymes. This card was cool and stylish with plain and simple wording – *Will you be my Valentine?* But then everything had changed so much recently, perhaps that included Grandad's taste in cards. I was kidding myself. An old person wouldn't choose a card like this and he would have signed it with his slightly shaky handwriting. It would have been a nice way for him to let me know he still loved me. This card was from someone else, and excitement mingled with disappointment inside me.

'Is there only one?' I asked as Em snuggled under the duvet with me.

'Only one for you, greedy guts,' she said slyly.

I pushed the card under my pillow. 'Who else has had a card then?' I tickled her under her armpits. 'Don't tell me it's Nick?'

'No,' she giggled. 'Mum and Dad have both got cards. I bet they sent them to each other. I think that's really nice.'

I smiled. It was better than nice, it was fantastic.

Laura was in conference with Daniel when I got to school. I walked straight past and pretended not to look, but I couldn't help noticing how his hair curled up slightly over his collar. Can you miss something you've never had? I was missing Daniel's friendship and we'd barely got past the acquaintance stage. There was an empty bench under the old oak tree in the furthest corner of the playground, so I claimed it for myself and got out a book. Everyone at home had obviously heard Dad shouting at me last night, although they didn't say anything. He had bellowed so loudly it was possible several people from school who lived within a half-mile radius might have heard as well. I didn't feel like talking to anyone except Laura. My head was down, eyes fixed on my book, and my rucksack was positioned in such a way that it took up the rest of the bench. Most normal, perceptive people would catch onto the fact that I wasn't in the mood to socialize, but the majority of teachers at my school wouldn't even get a pass if they took an exam in sensitivity to students.

'Is everything all right, Katrina?' Mrs Hawk hovered in front of me.

'Fine,' I mumbled, willing her to go away and leave me alone.

Some people just won't take a hint. She perched next to me on the bench arm, not speaking, just shuffling her books into some sort of order. I stared so hard at the words on my page they turned into a blur of zigzagging lines. She obviously wasn't going to move away. At last she won. Her silence forced the words out of me.

'Grandad's gone, Gran's moved into my bedroom, Mum's so busy with Gran she hasn't got any time for me, Dad's flipped but' – I glanced over at Laura and Daniel – 'apart from that everything's fine.'

She cast her know-all eyes across the playground. 'Have you and Laura fallen out?'

I buried my face in my scarf. 'No not really,' I said in a muffled voice.

She was quiet for a moment and I could almost hear her adding up the different thoughts and coming to a conclusion. I wished I'd kept my stupid mouth shut.

'I'm sorry your grandad's gone. I know you hoped he'd change his mind.' She edged a bit closer and I leaned away, trying not to make it look too obvious. 'I've got some news that might cheer you up.'

What was that? I wondered. Fractions had been voted as the utmost form of cruelty and were to be obliterated from the planet? Or, even better, perhaps the powers that be had decided maths was irrelevant after Year Six and should be subtracted from the curriculum. Somehow I didn't think this was what she was going to tell me.

'Can you keep a secret?'

I could see Laura giving me strange pitying glances. I pulled one of my most desperate, rescue-me expressions.

'I'm leaving.'

My first reaction was to think, Thank goodness, and then I realized she didn't just mean she was getting up from her claustrophobia-inducing position on the edge of my bench.

'Where are you going?' I thought of some other poor kids about to be tortured by her teaching and wondered if I should send them a warning.

'I'm not going to another school. I'm giving up teaching altogether.'

My eyes widened. Perhaps she'd been given the sack because of me. I must be her most famous failure as a pupil. Perhaps the head had decided she wasn't up to the job.

'Why?' I asked.

'It's time to do something different.'

She must have been able to read my thoughts. I didn't think teachers were capable of having any interests outside their own sad subjects.

'I trained as a teacher when my children were growing up, but I soon knew it was a mistake – teaching wasn't right for me. I couldn't give up because my husband became ill, but he's better now and I'm going to do what I've always wanted.'

'What's that?' I was really intrigued.

'I'm going to design and make my own jewellery.' She beamed at me and her seahorse earrings seemed to jiggle with delight. 'I've already got a couple of orders. I just needed something to make me take the plunge. You did that, Katrina.'

'Me?'

'When you stormed out of class that day, that was a turning point for me, and then talking about your grandad . . . it gave me the push I needed. If your grandad can take a chance, so can I.'

The bell rang for the start of the school day and she bounced up. 'Cheer up, Katrina, things are never as bad as they seem. Try to look on the bright side – at least you've only got me teaching you until the end of this term.'

I didn't know what to say but she ignored my embarrassment and just strode away towards her first lesson. I should have felt overjoyed; instead I felt a tiny bit sorry. I was positive I must be sickening for something.

* * *

'What was Mrs Hawk talking to you about?' It was first break and Laura was sitting on the science block steps.

'Nothing in particular,' I lied.

'It didn't look like it.'

'Grandad's actually gone,' I said, so matter-of-factly it felt as if I was telling her the time or reporting on something that happened thousands of years ago. 'I thought he might change his mind at the airport. I thought I'd be a good enough reason for him to stay, but obviously not.'

'Kat, I'm sorry' – she really sounded it too – 'but it doesn't work like that.'

It's strange how you really want something, and then when it's finally there, you wish for something different. At last Laura sounded as if she understood how I felt and her sympathy was cutting me apart.

'Don't be nice to me,' I gulped. Desperately I groped inside my frazzled brain for a change of subject. I picked one of the front runners out of the thoughts jostling for pole position.

'Did Daniel have anything to say this morning?' I knew it was a mistake as soon as the words escaped.

'About what?' She glanced at me curiously.

'Dunno.' I felt myself flushing under her gaze and stared into the distance, where Daniel just happened to be playing football. He looked over and caught my eye. My cheeks burned conspicuously.

'What's worse?' Laura asked as she studied her brother weaving towards the goal. 'Is it that period when you're waiting for them to go but they're still here, or is it when they've gone?'

'Both,' I said.

She nodded, not taking her eyes off Daniel. I couldn't take my eyes off him either.

'I thought so,' she said quietly.

I squeezed her cold fingers and she grabbed my hand.

'I'm sorry for not being a very good friend recently.'

'Me too,' I replied.

'We must try harder.' She mimicked Mrs Hawk's voice and I smiled.

'We must,' I agreed.

'Do you want to come roller-blading at half term?' she asked.

'That would be great,' I said.

'I'll see if Daniel wants to come too, shall I?'

'I – I don't think he'll be interested,' I stammered. 'You know what he thinks of me . . .'

'Mmm, I *do* know what he thinks of you' – her eyes twinkled mischievously – 'and I don't think he'll take much persuading.'

By now I must have looked as if I'd overdosed on a large quantity of red-hot chillis.

'At last my brother has realized what I've known for years.' She grinned at me. 'That you are a very special person.'

'I don't know where you got that idea from,' I muttered, trying to suppress the stupid grin that was spreading across my po-face.

'Really? So tell me about the Valentine card you got this morning.'

'How do you know I got one?'

She tilted her head on one side and gave me one of her meaningful looks.

'Did you send it for a joke?'

'Kat,' she sighed, 'are you being deliberately dense? Of course I didn't send it, but we both know who did.'

My heart felt as if it had done a much better forward roll than the ones I attempt during gym. I couldn't stop the grin any longer. My face ached with the force of it.

'Kat, he really likes you. Believe me.'

'That's typical timing,' I sighed. 'We start to become friends just as he's about to go away.'

'There's the telephone,' she said, 'and e-mail, and snail mail, and you could always come with me when I go and visit.'

'Hang on a minute,' I grimaced, 'you'll have us married next!'

'Well, there's a good idea,' she laughed.

'It's funny how things you expect to happen often don't,' I murmured, 'and the things you've never imagined in your wildest dreams *do*.'

'And sometimes people grow on you slowly,'

Laura said. 'When you're little you can't stand the taste of tea, then you start to like it a bit and by the time you're grown up you can't live without it! Perhaps you and Daniel will be like that!'

We burst out laughing, and as we stood up Laura linked her arm through mine. She guided me, blushing, past the football pitch, with my head down but my eyes drawn towards one player. He looked at me warily for a few seconds and then he grinned and he didn't care who saw. I smiled back, a sort of wobbly, wishy-washy, is-this-really-happening? sort of smile. For a few seconds I just thought about Daniel and me together. I forgot all about Grandad and I felt weird. I felt happy.

CHAPTER 18

Gran had spent the whole day tidying the house. Surfaces had been cleared, carpets hoovered, even the potpourri had been dusted. Nobody could find anything.

'I need to keep busy,' she said as Mum searched through the kitchen cupboards with gritted teeth, 'I've made a shopping list for food, and tomorrow I'm going to tackle the ironing. A man likes to come home to a nice tidy house, a good meal and crisp shirts.'

'Absolutely right.' Dad smiled and poured three glasses of red wine.

Mum made a sort of snorting noise like a dragon working up to a frenzy of fire-breathing while furiously mashing some potatoes to a pulp.

'I've never had sleepless nights about your developing repetitive strain injury from too much housework, that's for sure.' Dad patted Mum on the bum. He'd obviously gulped his wine and it had affected that part of his brain that controls discretion and self-preservation. Gran laughed, a tinkling sound that I hadn't heard for ages. It seemed wrong that she should be laughing so soon after Grandad had gone.

Mum extricated the potato masher from the saucepan and moved ominously towards Dad. Her face was grim, with her eyes narrowed viciously and her mouth as mean as a pantomime villain. Nick, Em and I exchanged glances, all of us deciding it was time to take cover at the same moment. Suddenly Mum put on a spurt, backing Dad into a corner. I closed my eyes for a moment, waiting for the usual blazing row, when I heard Dad laugh. Then Mum laughed too – in fact everyone was laughing. I opened my eyes to see Dad flecked with blobs of potato. They were all over his face, in his hair and splattered on his shirt. He wiped one of the blobs onto his finger and put it on the end of Mum's nose. Then he wrapped his arms around her and kissed her on the lips. She flopped against him like the old days and he squeezed her so tightly and kissed her for so long I became worried she'd suffocate.

'See,' Nick whispered, 'I told you they'd be fine, told you it was just a phase.'

'One kiss doesn't mean they're on course for their silver wedding,' I muttered, not wanting to admit he was right again, but I did feel all warm and safe. I did sense the crisis had passed.

When the phone rang nobody moved for a few seconds.

'I'll get it,' Dad said at last as he and Mum un-wound themselves.

Gran had already set the table, which was usually my job, and she seemed to be taking charge of the cooking too. I was quickly coming to the conclusion that giving up my bedroom was a sacrifice worth making.

Dad came back into the room and ran towards me. Before I could stop him he'd lifted me up under my arms and swung me around as if I was only Em's size. The wine must have given him some extra strength too. 'You've done it!' he laughed.

'What?' I asked. 'Given you a hernia?'

'You've been offered a place in the under-fourteen England table-tennis squad. The selector was so impressed with the way you pulled back from defeat in the last match, she wants to give you a chance.'

I think everyone clapped their hands and squealed except me. I'd barely thought about the table tennis, I was so convinced I'd blown my chances. I felt stunned. Emma smothered me with hugs, Mum danced all around the kitchen, still with a potato-decorated nose, and Nick just beamed at me. Gran was smiling too, but she looked slightly sad and sank quietly onto a chair.

I'd always dreamed of how I'd feel at this moment, imagined the pure elation that would overcome me. The first thing I'd planned to do was go and tell Grandad. I wasn't going to talk to him over the phone but face to face so we could touch each other's happiness. At this moment I didn't even know where he was, apart from being somewhere in Spain. There was no way of contacting him even if I'd wanted to, and I wasn't sure I did. Dad cracked open some chilled champagne he'd been keeping in the fridge 'for just this moment' and I felt like a party pooper at someone's birthday. All I could think about was the one person who should have been there to share the moment with me and wasn't. It was as if he'd stolen some of my pleasure, packed it in his suitcase and taken it with him, and it made me so, so angry.

'To Katy!' They all raised their glasses.

'And Grandad,' Nick said quietly. I should have been the one to say it but he knew I couldn't. Perhaps he shouldn't have either. The atmosphere in the kitchen plummeted as fast as a lift with its cables cut. I glared at him, but he had that stubborn look on his face that means there's no way he's going to change course. 'It's a pity we can't phone to tell him the good news, isn't it, Kat?'

I wished the kitchen floor would open up and Nick would fall down a gaping hole to shut him up.

'Gran can tell him when she goes to visit,' Em piped up. I wanted to throttle her too. Gran looked as if she was going to cry. 'You *are* going to visit him, aren't you, Gran?' Em scrambled onto Gran's knee. 'We'll visit Great-Grandma lots and lots while you're away so she won't be sad.'

'Don't give her any more sips of champagne,' I hissed at Dad. 'She doesn't know what she's saying.'

'I don't know, Emma,' Gran said, staring at the bubbles in her glass, 'I hadn't thought about it. I suppose I could go and visit him if he wanted me to.' She looked up at all of us. 'Couldn't I?'

Nobody answered. It had seemed so final when Grandad left; suddenly I realized it wasn't final at all. It wasn't like getting to the end of a book, finding out what happened and putting it in your bookshelf, never to be opened again. This story was going to carry on indefinitely, whether I liked it or not, twisting and turning with all the hurt and happiness bound together.

'I've had an idea,' Gran said, gathering herself together and putting a determinedly bright expression on her face. 'I'll cook Katrina a special celebratory meal tomorrow. What would you like, dear?'

'Chicken,' I said, 'and . . .'

'Some of my home-made chips?' Gran smiled.

I nodded uncertainly. 'That would be lovely, Gran,' I said.

The champagne fizzed busily under my nose, the bubbles tickled the inside of my mouth and danced down my throat. I didn't know whether I was ready for chips again, but there was only one way to find out. I felt like a totally different person to the one who had sat at Gran's kitchen table just over two weeks ago. Everything had happened so fast I didn't feel like me anymore. I wondered if I'd ever get used to the new person under my outer shell. The champagne made me feel brave. I saw Nick watching me.

'I want to make a toast too,' I said, standing on a stool and swaying. 'I want to toast all my family and friends who have supported me.' I saw Nick urging me on. 'I want to toast Grandad too, because I wouldn't be here without him.' It wasn't the most effusive speech, but it was the best I could manage.

It had been a huge effort. Everyone was quiet. You could have heard the potato splodges drop off Dad's shirt. I wanted to say I wished Grandad happiness in his new home, but I couldn't manage that and I thought it might have been a bit insensitive with Gran sitting there. We all raised our glasses and drank a silent, tearful toast to the family, the old one and the new.

'Will you write to Grandad, as soon as we've got an address?' Nick sat down beside me while everyone else dished up the supper.

'Maybe.'

'You ought to.'

'OK, there's no need to nag. I'll do it.'

He looked satisfied with my answer. I'll do it in my own time, I thought. When I'm ready. The trouble was, I didn't know when that would be. It could be months or years or never. I had no idea. Nothing was certain any more, least of all how I would feel from one moment to the next. I hoped Grandad would write to me first and then maybe I would write back. Eventually.